16,000 Suspects

Suspects

A RAGBRAI Mystery

Edited by Barbara Lounsberry

Commissioned by Public Radio KUNI

16,000 Suspects, A RAGBRAI Mystery
Barbara Lounsberry, Editor
Kim Behm, Illustrator
Amy Roach, Designer
Gregory Shanley, Project Director
Jons Olsson, Project Finance/Marketing Director

ISBN 0-9662041-2-3

Published by Public Radio KUNI

University of Northern Iowa
Cedar Falls, Iowa 50613-0359

Special Thanks

KUNI thanks The Des Moines Register and Tribune Company for permission to use the name RAGBRAI® for this book. Editor Barbara Lounsberry deserves the thanks for coming up with the brilliant idea of using RAGBRAI®, also known as the "Register's Annual Great Bicycle Ride Across Iowa," as the setting for this murder/mystery. The Des Moines Register and Tribune Company gave not only permission, but supported the creative efforts of the 17 authors by placing few restrictions on the writing. The "Register's Annual Great Bicycle Ride Across Iowa" is an event in which all Iowans take pride.

Editor's note: There has never been a murder on RAGBRAI® and let's hope there never will be. It is a unique and wonderful event on many levels. While great pains were taken to make sure the writers created a realistic story, it is still a work of fiction. The RAGBRAI® of "16,000 Suspects" is obviously somewhat skewed from reality due to the murder that takes place, and the concerns which naturally follow. It is KUNI's hope that RAGBRAI® in reality continues as the outstanding Iowa event that it is.

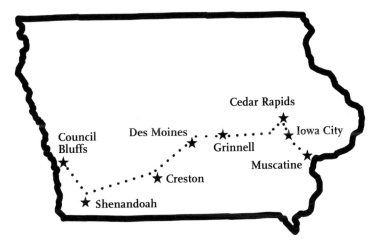

The fictional RAGBRAI route
that serves as the backdrop
for KUNI's
"16,000 Suspects:
A RAGBRAI Mystery"

Contents

Foreword

There is no doubt about it: writers are one of the nicest groups of people with whom to work. When KUNI published its first murder mystery, *Time & Chance*, in 1998, I thought fate had smiled and led me not only to 17 talented Iowa witers, but also to bright, creative, caring, proud, and thoughtful individuals as well.

Extraordinarily, this new novel, *16,000 Suspects: A RAGBRAI Mystery*, is the work of 17 different Iowa writers, but they have proven just as skilled and considerate as the first. And that is saying a lot. Last year, many of the *Time & Chance* writers attended book signings and public speaking events on the project. There was no financial reward involved; they just wanted to go the extra step to help KUNI make its fundraising project a success. I did not expect that kind of dedication from the *Time & Chance* writers, and I certainly do not expect it from our current totally new group of talented Iowa writers who have created *16,000 Suspects*. Nevertheless, they have been equally generous and thoughtful. Not one has missed a deadline—and most had only a week or less to draft their chapters—and many passed on useful character and plot comments to help those that followed them.

16,000 Suspects, like *Time & Chance*, is unusual in that it was written primarily by e-mail. Chuck Offenburger, the long-time "Iowa Boy" columnist for *The Des Moines Register* and a RAGBRAI regular, created the opening chapter scenario and selected the fictional route for the novel's RAGBRAI, which is set in the year 2000. RAGBRAI XXVIII, as you will see, travels from Council Bluffs to Shenandoah, Creston, Des Moines, Grinnell, Cedar Rapids, and Iowa City before ending with a splash (and the mystery's resolution) in Muscatine. Along the way, our writers stop and pay homage to many other Iowa towns and sites, including Villisca, Winterset and *The Bridges of Madison County*, Cumming, and the Amanas.

Chuck Offenburger not only wrote the opening chapter, but he provided Editor Barbara Lounsberry and the other 16 writers with background informaton on RAGBRAI's history and lore. Throughout the novel's composition he served as an ever-ready resource, supplying on request route particulars (which back roads?) and color. Occasionally, perhaps, the writers have taken poetic license with Iowa's landscape—the road from Shenandoah to Essex may in reality be a bit flatter than it is in *16,000 Suspects*. However, by and large our authors have done their research—several biked or drove their day's route—and have stayed true to the Iowa settings while weaving their beguiling fictional yarn.

As with *Time & Chance*, when a chapter was due, it was e-mailed to Editor Barbara Lounsberry, a UNI professor of English. She edited the chapter and e-mailed it on to me, to our book designer Amy Roach, and to the other authors. As with *Time & Chance*, we did not create the novel's characters in advance because we wanted to allow the writers as much freedom as we could. In spite of this avowal, *16,000 Suspects* became a highly collaborative endeavor—and we think this greater collaboration shows.

Because *16,000 Suspects* unfolds across the week of RAGBRAI, Barbara Lounsberry found herself being more directive. "We're on day 4 (Wednesday) and we're in Grinnell," she would e-mail an author, or "We've got to get the rolling festival moving." But the best collaboration came from the writers themselves. Early on a group of writers suggested politely via e-mail that we would have a more satisfying novel if the writers agreed from the beginning "whodunit" and why. Barbara polled the writers and this recommendaton gained wide support. Knowing who committed the murder and why would actually free the writers to layer in red herrings and dramatic irony, many assured us. We hope you agree that this more collaborative approach succeeds, and we want to give special thanks to Max Allan Collins for suggesting the murderer and motive.

KUNI thanks *The Des Moines Register* for allowing us to use the

licensed name RAGBRAI in this novel. Barbara Lounsberry came
up with the brilliant idea of using RAGBRAI—also known as The
Des Moines Register's Great Bike Ride Across Iowa—as the setting
for this murder mystery.

Publishing a book and getting people to buy it takes a lot of help.
KUNI wants to thank the University of Northern Iowa Graduate College
for providing funds to help pay the writers. Cedar Falls artist Kim
Behm did his usual terrific job in creating the book's cover. If 16,000
Suspects jumps off the store shelves as we hope, a good deal of the
credit goes to the eye-catching cover Kim has produced, as well as
the highly-readable text designed by Amy Roach. How many books
come with their own bookmarks? I also want to thank Barbara
Lounsberry for her contributions as editor which included editing
for continuity and titling several chapters as well as suggesting the
RAGBRAI theme.

I was not sure Barbara could equal the job she did on *Time &
Chance*, but you will see she rose to the challenge. My wife, Sonya
Shanley, and KUNI Administrative Assistant Barbara Reid helped
proofread the novel, as did Vince Gotera an Associate Professor of
English at UNI and Frances Lounsberry of Cedar Falls. We want to
extend our great thanks to them for their assistance. Jons Olsson,
KUNI's Assistant Director of Broadcasting, made sure we kept our
spending down, handled promotion, and selected the novel's title.

As we learned from the first book we published, *Moments in Iowa
History*, which sold out, as well as from our first murder mystery,
Time & Chance, creating a book is just the first step. Filling orders by
mail, creating promotional material, and getting the book in stores
is the work that really makes or breaks these projects. KUNI can
undertake these unique projects (for a public radio station) because
of the talent and determination of its staff. Thank you all!

Greg Shanley
KUNI News Director
Book Project Director

Disclaimer

"16,000 Suspects: A RAGBRAI® Mystery" is a work of fiction written by its authors and is not a work created by the Des Moines Register and Tribune Company. The characters and events in this book are inventions of its authors and do not depict any real persons or events. RAGBRAI® is a registered trademark of and licensed by the Des Moines Register and Tribune Company. The marks and names, RAGBRAI®, RAGBRAI® XXVII, RIDE RIGHT®, and "Register's Annual Great Bicycle Ride Across Iowa," are and shall be the exclusive property of the Des Moines Register and Tribune Company. These marks are used by the authors with the written permission of the Des Moines Register and Tribune Company.

The Des Moines Register and Tribune Company has exercised no control over the cover art or fictional content and therefore makes no claim as to its accuracy of fact or portrayal of the experience of RAGBRAI®.

For the record, no suspicious deaths have occurred during the 27 years of the ride. Approximately 8,500 full-week applications and 1,500 day-ride applications (per day) are accepted to participate in RAGBRAI® each year. For a complete history of RAGBRAI®, or further information about this annual Iowa event, please contact the RAGBRAI® office: by phone: 1-800-I RIDE IA (474-3342) or 515-284-8282, by mail: P.O. Box 622, Des Moines, IA 50303-0622, on the web: www.ragbrai.org

I

Iowa is not Flat

By Chuck Offenburger

It is the year 2010 now, a full decade after it happened. Enough healing time has passed that we can finally report and reflect on what the media called the "Cycle-pathic Murders" on RAGBRAI XXVIII in the year 2000.

They were, of course, the first murders ever on that grand, old Iowa institution of RAGBRAI—the Des Moines Register's Annual Great Bicycle Ride Across Iowa. It shocked the state, intrigued the nation, and probably still gives the willies to the 10,000 cyclists who were participating that summer.

They'd come from all 50 states and 14 other countries for a weeklong vacation on bicycles. What brought them was RAGBRAI's reputation for being an innocent, if rigorous, romp across Iowa. It had long since become the biggest, oldest, and, most agreed, best bicycle touring event in the world. RAGBRAI had always been a veritable rolling folk festival, staffed by a half-dozen paid employees of the *Des Moines Register* and by thousands of volunteers, those ever-so-hospitable Iowans on the farms and in the small towns and cities along the route.

The riders came expecting pork burgers, sweet corn, pie, music, lemonade, ice cream, more pie, a few beers—and lots and lots of fun over a 475-mile, seven-day ride from the Missouri River to the Mississippi.

They sure didn't expect to become involved in one of the most famous murder investigations the Iowa State Patrol ever mounted. It made the national news for seven consecutive days since NBC-TV had coincidentally sent a *Today Show* crew to cover RAGBRAI as the network had done once before, in 1987.

As always, the Patrol had dispatched a dozen of its Safety Education Officers to provide security and traffic control for one of Iowa's best-known tourism events. These officers were usually veteran State Troopers who, after years "on the road" in Iowa, were carefully selected to do safety programs and public relations in schools and for other civic organizations. The last full week of July each summer they became the good-natured cops who had a remarkable record of getting thousands of people safely across Iowa on bicycles. They'd looked on it as happy duty.

Yes, there had been 16 deaths on RAGBRAI during its first 25 years, but only one of those happened in a bicycle accident and the others happened as a result of medical problems. When you consider that 167,150 people had participated on the ride in that time, the safety record was indeed impressive.

But on that fateful RAGBRAI in 2000, in the middle of the night after the first day's ride, the State Patrol was thrown into double duty. When the body of a middle-aged male cyclist was discovered in a burning pup tent in a small campground set up in Priest Park in the heart of Shenandoah in southwest Iowa—and when it was immediately obvious this was a homicide—the Troopers quickly became detectives.

The next morning, some members of the public and a few cyclists called for the rest of RAGBRAI XXVIII to be canceled. But the *Register's* executives and the RAGBRAI staff respected the counsel of the Patrol to have the ride continue. The cyclists, after all, had come from far-flung points to spend a week in Iowa; the towns along the way were all prepared, and as the Troopers said, to end the ride would mean that the possible murderer or murderers and potential witnesses would scatter far and wide. It would be better, all agreed, for the ride to roll on across Iowa.

Over the next six days, the State Patrol, with assistance from other law enforcement agencies along the way, put together one of the most fascinating—and public—murder investigations ever conducted in Iowa.

And it came with a cliffhanger of an ending, one so stunning that some reporters wondered among themselves if the Patrol was faking it. When the Troopers spotted their chief suspect in the big crowd of cyclists at RAGBRAI's official closing ceremonies on the Mississippi River bank in Muscatine, they made a dramatic arrest that was followed immediately by a heartfelt confession. And that let thousands of people go home with a sense of closure to a crazy week in their lives, one they will never, ever forget.

It was a week that started with high spirits in Council Bluffs where the campground and headquarters were established on the neighboring campuses of the Iowa School for the Deaf and Lewis Central High School. Overnight stops were planned in Shenandoah, Creston, Des Moines, Grinnell, Cedar Rapids and Iowa City before the finish in Muscatine.

By mid-afternoon of the opening Saturday, thousands of riders were already at the Bluffs campgrounds. Friends who hadn't seen each other since the previous RAGBRAI greeted each other like they were part of some huge high school class reunion. They ranged in age from infants who would ride in lightweight mini-trailers behind their parents' bicycles and children under 10 who would ride their own bikes, to senior citizens in their 70s and 80s. The big bicycle clubs, with hundreds of members, arrived on charter buses with Ryder rental trucks carrying their bikes, duffel bags, and camping equipment: the Des Moines Cycle Club; the Quad-City Bike Club; "BIC" (Bicyclists of Iowa City); the Rainbow Cyclists from Waterloo and Cedar Falls; the Hawkeye Pedalers from Cedar Rapids; the Pott Pedalers from Pottawattamie County (Council Bluffs area); the North Jersey Touring Club from just west of New York City; and others.

Groups of friends came as teams with colorful names— Team Skunk from the Des Moines and Ames areas, taking their name from the Skunk River; "The Whiners" from Michigan; Team Bad Boy from Colorado; Team FART ("Friends All Riding Together") from Des Moines; the "Rogues of the Night" from Iowa City; the "High Rollers" from Las Vegas; the lavish eaters of "Team Gourmet" from Chicago; "Team Escape from New York," a merry band of police officers and firefighters from New York City; the "Nooners" from Des Moines; Team Mary from Waterloo and Cedar Falls; and more. The cyclists were making last-minute purchases from bicycle shops operating from Winnebago campers and vans, with each of the shops selling specially designed RAGBRAI XXVIII T-shirts. Mechanics—some professionals and more of them amateurs—were fine-tuning bicycles that ranged in value from a few dollars to $5,000 and more.

Most of the cyclists stopped at the *Register's* campground headquarters, a couple of vans around a sales booth that offered newspapers and RAGBRAI souvenirs. Mainly they stopped there to pay homage to the self-described "Grampa RAGBRAI," John Karras, the 70-year-old former *Register* columnist who was co-founder of the ride and still its host.

"RAGBRAI certainly has not been all of my life, but it's been a very large part of it," Karras wrote the previous year when he collaborated with his photographer-cyclist-wife Ann Karras on a book about the ride. "It's been a marvelous gift, conceived in innocence, achieved through happenstance and continuing in the unlikeliest of magical manners."

RAGBRAI coordinator Jim Green, 60, was also there, handling a thousand small details and getting ready to direct the event for the ninth year.

"Think safety!" Green yelled to rider after rider. "Be sure to wear your helmet."

The RAGBRAI rookies—or "Virgins," as they often call themselves—were surrounding older veterans, asking them for advice. The man most sought was Frank "Huck" Thompson, 63, the former *Des Moines Register* mailroom employee who after 27 years of RAGBRAI was the only cyclist who had ridden every mile every year.

We watched as Thompson, surrounded by the newcomers on "Team Bella" from northeast Iowa, told them that "one of the most important things you can do on this ride is get out of that tent in the morning, stretch and sing, 'Zipadee doo dah, zipadee aay, my oh my, what a wonderful day!'"

And he sang it real loud!

"I've been reading about you since I was a little girl," Charlotte "Charlie" Andropolous, 27, the coordinator of Team Bella, told Thompson. "Can I get my picture taken with you?"

She explained that she ran a bed and breakfast near Bella, the town of 3,997 people on the Mississippi, but that she also was a part-time correspondent in that area for the *Des Moines Register*. She told Thompson she would be watching for vignettes on the ride to supplement John Karras' stories.

"I'm always good for a quote, Sweetheart," Thompson cracked.

And indeed he has been.

Rock music throbbed all afternoon and evening there in Council Bluffs. The mid-afternoon temperature hit 91 degrees, but nobody seemed to mind. It just kept the "Beverage Garden" (RAGBRAI officially discourages "Beer Gardens") and the soft drink and ice cream stands busy.

The Lewis Central Athletic and Music Booster Clubs joined forces to put on a spaghetti dinner that packed the school gym for hours. Restaurants all over the Council Bluffs and Omaha areas were jammed with people arriving for the bike ride. Back at the campgrounds, there were Protestant and Catholic church services in the high school auditorium, conducted by local clergy with help from ordained ministers and priests who also happened to be RAGBRAI riders.

Signs on store windows and on service stations all over the metropolitan area welcomed the cyclists and cheered them toward the week's challenge: "God Speed and Tailwinds, RAGBRAI!," "Muscatine or Bust," "Iowa is NOT flat!".

Sunday's 65-mile ride to Shenandoah proved to first-time visitors to Iowa that the state is definitely not flat. They had to ride over the spectacular Loess Hills immediately after leaving Council Bluffs, and then they found themselves in the rolling hills of southwest Iowa.

But temperatures were surprisingly mild with a high of 82. Winds were from the northwest and thus favorable, and the day turned into a delightful cruise. Church groups and 4-H clubs set up snack and drink stands along the way. The fastest of the cyclists were arriving in Shenandoah by the time local folks were leaving their church services and, by early afternoon, the town was in enthusiastic gridlock.

West Sheridan Avenue, which is the main street in the town of 6,000, was closed to vehicular traffic and given over completely to the visiting cyclists. The curbs were lined with food and drink stands. The beverage garden was full, and so were the taverns. The Masons and the Knights of Columbus went together and hosted a very popular turkey and noodles dinner in the Liberty Memorial Building, an elegant old community center that was the World War II-era National Guard Armory.

High Heel and the Sneakers, an Omaha rock band that had delighted the RAGBRAI riders in the 1980s, had come back together for a reunion performance on a specially-built stage at downtown Shenandoah's main intersection where five streets come together. Thousands of happy visitors there surrounded the old silver-painted municipal water fountain, 10 feet tall and three feet square with a neon sign on top saying the fountain was sponsored by the Women's Christian Temperance Union. Most of the cyclists were too young to have known of the WCTU and were clueless to the cruel irony of all the beer drinking going on around it.

Most local people said it was the best night in Shenandoah since the summer of 1986 when the Everly Brothers, charter members of the Rock 'n' Roll Hall of Fame, came back to the town where they went to high school and performed before a crowd of 8,000. A few older Shenandoahans begged to differ, saying it was the best night since the late, great Earl May, the nurseryman and radio station operator, used to host Harvest Jubilees in the 1930s and '40s.

On this RAGBRAI night, the street dance closed down at 11 p.m., per the orders of the *Register's* RAGBRAI staff. They'd discovered over the years that if the music stops at that hour, the bike riders will get back to their tents and get a fair night's rest before trying to ride the next day. An extra hour of late-night music, fun, and drinking can cause trouble.

But despite the orderly end to official RAGBRAI activities downtown, there was indeed trouble. At 3 a.m., the phone rang in the Tall Corn Motel room of Lt. Scott Dallas, the commander of the Iowa State Patrol Troopers on the ride.

"Is it already 4:30 a.m.?" said the groggy Dallas as he answered the phone.

"Unfortunately, Lieutenant, this isn't your wake-up call," said Shenandoah Police Chief Davey James. "Well, maybe it is a wake-up call. At any rate, we've got a fatality. A bunch of your bikers chased down one of our officers and asked him to come to Priest Park. They said there'd been a fire in one of the tents. You better meet me there right away."

Ten minutes later, Dallas and three other Troopers—Lt. Gary Hassell from Mount Pleasant, Trooper Lars Loving from Cedar Falls, and the old veteran Trooper Bill Zenith from Red Oak—were in uniform and leaving the motel.

When they got to the park, located two blocks south of downtown, they saw two Shenandoah police cars with red lights revolving. An eerily quiet crowd of about 200 sleepy RAGBRAI riders stood in a wide circle around the charred fragments of a tent that had been set up away from the others there in the park.

Police Chief James waved Lt. Dallas and the other troopers to the front of the tent.

"Get ready," the chief said.

He pulled back the tattered flap. Lt. Dallas looked inside. Neither James's earlier briefing nor anything he'd encountered working a dozen previous RAGBRAIs prepared him for what he saw.

"Sweet Jesus!" he gasped. "I can't believe this!"

CHUCK OFFENBURGER *is Writer-in-Residence at Buena Vista University in Storm Lake, Iowa, and a columnist for* The Iowan Magazine. *He is a native of Shenandoah, a graduate of Vanderbilt University in Nashville, Tenn., and for 26 years was a reporter and columnist for the* Des Moines Register. *While there, he served as co-host of RAGBRAI with John Karras. After leaving the Register in 1998, Chuck and his wife, Carla Offenburger, joined the faculty and staff of Buena Vista. Chuck is the author of three books:* Iowa Boy: Ten Years of Columns; Babe: an Iowa Legend, *a biography of Des Moines restauranteur Babe Bisignano; and* Ah, You Iowans! At Home, At Work, At Play, at War, *a collection of columns. He is currently completing a biography of Iowa business leader Bill Krause, titled* Don't Look Back: We're Not Headed That Way.

2

Ditched

By Ed Gorman

I probably set a record that first day of RAGBRAI. No, I'm not talking about speed records. Or mileage records.

I'm talking about falling-in-love records.

When a balding, slightly overweight, somewhat nearsighted and recently-dumped forty-eight-year-old mystery writer gets around so many attractive, healthy females, falling in love is something you just can't avoid.

Not that any of my gaga-eyed gazes had been returned. Not only don't I look like a movie star, I don't act like one either. After twenty-one years of marriage, I'd forgotten how to flirt. I'd read a lot of self-help books about dating since Amy dumped me for the family podiatrist, but I hadn't yet read the one on flirting.

By the end of the first day, I was worn out. Dinner for me was potato salad, a fish sandwich with plenty of goop, and as much Diet Pepsi as I could guzzle without ruining my Cary Grant image.

I ate at a big picnic table with about twenty other exuberantly exhausted riders. Sundown was a brilliant gold and red and buff blue. The winds dried our sweaty bodies and promised good sleeping weather.

Eyepatch sat next to me, unfortunately.

I called him Eyepatch because I didn't know his name. I didn't want to know his name, either.

We'd ridden together for a couple of long stretches and all he did was complain. He didn't like the way RAGBRAI was organized; he didn't like a lot of the riders, and he thought the Iowa countryside was flat and uninteresting. He didn't say where he was from, and I didn't ask.

You know the kind. He seems to take great pleasure in spoiling everybody else's fun. The more unhappy you are, the happier he is.

The one thing that bothered me especially were his knives: two sixteen-inch pearl-handled switchblades that fell out of his backpack when he took a small spill on some sand earlier in the day.

These weren't clean-your-fingernails knives. These were killer knives. They were such killer knives, in fact, they were illegal.

"You like to sword fight, do you?" I'd said as he tucked them back into his backpack.

"You're not funny." And that was all he'd said.

The eyepatch was mysterious. It covered his right eye. With his graying hair and hawk nose, it lent him a certain manly drama. But his bitchiness took it all away.

"I wonder if they've ever heard of cold pop in this state," he said now, at dinner time.

By this time, I wasn't paying a lot of attention. At least for the moment, I'd managed to interest a lovely fortyish woman in my story. Not about Amy. You should never lead with a story about being dumped for a podiatrist. But about being a mystery writer. A lot of people think writing is a romantic occupation.

"As soon as I get back to Cedar Falls," she said, "I'm going to buy a couple of your books."

"You won't have to. I'll send you some."

"Really? Will you sign them?"

"Sure."

"I've got a lot more reading time since my husband and I split up. In fact, that's what I do most nights."

"You try those hamburgers?" Eyepatch said. "I'll probably get food poisoning. There's a plot for you, Mr. Mystery Writer."

"You don't seem to be having a very good time," Jennie Wyman said to Eyepatch. "I think you just need to get adjusted to the regimen."

Eyepatch frowned. "A bunch of hayseeds trying to prove they're still young. That's the regimen."

Jennie laughed. "Wasn't I married to you once?"

Eyepatch kept right on frowning.

And then his cell phone rang.

Shenandoah was close enough to a transmitter for cell phones.

Eyepatch snapped his phone on and said, "It's about time."
Then he got up and walked away, talking angrily into the
phone as he walked.

"Friend of yours?" Jennie said.

"A friend of all mankind's."

She smiled. "I always feel sorry for people like him. For a
while. Then I start really disliking them."

"I guess I passed by the feel sorry part real fast and went
right to the dislike. Intense dislike."

We went for a walk. The stars came out. Everything got
lazy and cozy, settling in for the night.

We walked down by a deep and fast-running creek. There
were weeping willows and nightbirds and a distant owl.

Jennie said, "This is nice."

"Yeah. It is." I decided to say it. I hadn't said anything
like this since I was wooing Amy back in the days when the
ROTC building in Iowa City got burned down. You know,
the good old days. The marijuana diet and all the depress-
ing music you could stand. "What's really nice is meeting
you."

"I was going to say the same thing but I was chicken."

"I'm known for valor."

"Uh-huh."

A hour-and-a-half had passed. We decided to walk back.
It was a firefly summer with the smell of new mown grass
on the full moon night.

This time, she was the brave one. She slid her arm through
mine and gave me a kind of sliding hug on my shoulder. In

these days of XXX videos that probably doesn't seem like much. But my heart was racing and my mind was thinking all sorts of cornball recently-dumped romantic thoughts. I'd met somebody. It'd probably end when RAGBRAI was over—or maybe even sooner—but for right now I was just going to enjoy it.

"Well," she said, "I'm sharing a tent with a girl friend of mine. See you in the morning."

"See you in the morning," I said.

And walked over to where my bike and bedroll awaited me. There was nobody else around. A lot of people were still out having fun. The swine.

Eyepatch had set up his tent before we'd walked down to the park for dinner. It was set in a nook of oaks.

I rolled out my bedroll at an angle from his—many yards away—and fell into a contented sleep. Only a few hours passed, however, when the excited barks of a dog awakened me. I looked around and saw the faint play of flames inside Eyepatch's tent.

It wasn't the flickering of a Coleman. It appeared to be real fire. And it was now eating through the exterior wall of the small pup tent.

I ran over there. My footsteps must have scared off the dog who came leaping out from the tent and ran away into the darkness.

Maybe Eyepatch had fallen asleep and the uninvited dog had knocked over a lantern or candle and set everything on fire.

I flung the tent flap back.

By now, the flames were completely enclosing the tent. It was an oven.

I did the only thing I could. I shouted again and again for him to wake up. And then I put my hands inside and started to drag him out by the ankles.

His hair and his shirt were on fire and ordinarily a guy would be screaming pretty loud by this time.

But Eyepatch wouldn't ever scream again.

Standing up from each eye was a pearl-handled switchblade. Driven deep and bloody.

ED GORMAN'S *most recent novel is* The Day the Music Died, *a mystery set in the imaginary Iowa town of Black River Falls in 1959. The book takes place in the 48 hours following the crash of rock 'n' roll singer Buddy Holly's plane. Novelist Carolyn See wrote of the novel in* The Washington Post: *"Our hero loves [his town] . . . and readers should love it, too!"* The New York Times *said, "The little town in the Iowa heartland stirs to life at Ed Gorman's affectionate touch." Gorman, an Iowa native, attended Coe College in Cedar Rapids and worked in advertising for twenty years. He is the author of twenty novels and five collections of short stories. His Iowa-based novella,* Moonchasers, *has just been optioned as a feature film by Ally McBeal co-star Gil Bellows. Gorman is married to novelist Carol Gorman.*

3
"16,000 Suspects"

By Barbara Collins

Lt. Scott Dallas—a lean, raw-boned thirty-eight, crisp as the pre-dawn morning air in his trooper browns—stretched his arms to the clear starry sky. Had anyone been watching, they might have thought he was mimicking the lighted motel sign behind him, the massive ear of lightbulb corn that reached skyward above the Tall Corn Motel.

Looking very much like an Indian with his sharp cheekbones and narrow dark eyes, Dallas did not feel the least bit crisp himself. After the rock concert (the opening act, Cruisin', was fantastic), he had sat up till 2 a.m. drinking beer and talking RAGBRAI's past with his fellow troopers, all veterans of the bike ride. He had just gotten to sleep when the phone roused him.

From the motel room door behind Dallas, another trooper emerged, shambling toward the Iowa State Patrol commander, tucking his shirt in with one hand, hat in the other. Lt. Gary Hassell, a pouchy-eyed, paunchy forty-two, looked like the unmade bed he'd left behind.

"You look like I feel," Dallas told his roommate.

"Coffee," Hassell said. "Coffee first, then we can swap smart-ass repartee."

"Repartee?" somebody said, down the way.

It was Lars Loving, a twenty-something trooper who fancied himself a blond Tom Cruise type (only if the lights were very dim and you really squinted, Dallas thought) looking every bit as crisp as Dallas but obviously feeling much better.

"You musta took some classes at Wesleyan," Loving said, "to pick up such a high-class vocabulary."

"Coffee," Hassell mumbled his mantra.

Bringing up the rear was Loving's motel roommate, Bill Zenith, bucket-headed, stocky, fiftyish. He was shuffling, too, and looked like he might have slept in his uniform.

"There's a convenience store," Zenith said, rubbing his eyes, "on the way to that park. They aren't usually open all night, but 'cause of the shindig, we should be able to get Hassell his caffeine transfusion."

"First thing Bill does when he hits a town," Loving said, "is scope out the doughnut landscape. Within minutes of entering a new locale, his keen deductive powers lead him to—"

Zenith said something colorfully foul, and they all laughed—except for Dallas.

"Kid's got a point, Bill," Hassell said. "You're a walkin' cliché. Confirmin' everybody's suspicion about cops and doughnuts."

"Confirm this," Zenith said good-naturedly, with a gesture they all understood and laughed at. Except Dallas.

"Get the jollies out of your system, girls," Dallas told them. "When we get to that park, it's no laughing matter."

Suddenly sobered, the four troopers stood facing each other in the parking lot which was washed in moon- and starlight in the shadow of the tall corn sign.

"Guess this'll be a RAGBRAI to remember," Loving said, but he wasn't smiling.

"Kinda beats hell outa the RAGBRAI yarns we were swappin' last night," Zenith said, heel of one hand on his holstered sidearm.

"Wait till you hear the details," Dallas said. He hadn't shared the bizarre circumstances—the double knives to the eyes, the burning of the victim . . . .

"Coffee first." Hassell held up a hand. "Coffee first. Then grisly details. Please, coffee . . . ."

They sipped their steaming coffee and ate their doughnuts—incredibly fresh, still warm, and so delicious—sitting in Dallas' patrol car, which for RAGBRAI duty he was sharing with Hassell. Loving and Zenith's patrol car was parked alongside in the otherwise empty convenience store lot. The commander wanted to fill his men in; no rush getting to the scene—the Shenandoah cops had it covered, and the corpse wasn't going anywhere.

"Goddamn brutal," Loving said from the backseat. The smartass kid had turned pale; he alone of the veteran cops had lost his appetite, his doughnut untouched.

"You gonna eat that or not?" Zenith asked.

"Take it," Loving said, shivering, shuddering, handing the glazed doughnut over to the older trooper.

"Is it ritualistic, you think?" Hassell asked, a new man with coffee pumped into him. "Knives through the eyes. Some kinda Satanic practice?"

"We're going to have that run through the national crime data base," Dallas said, "see if it connects up with anything."

Hassell said, "Yeah, but the big question is—do we pull the plug on the big bike ride?"

"Shut down RAGBRAI?" Loving asked, wide-eyed. "That's Un-American."

"Un-Iowan, anyway," Zenith grunted, through a bite of doughnut.

Dallas sipped his coffee. "Davey James, the police chief, has the crime scene secured; he's already called the D.C.I. to get a full rolling lab in here, to go over that charred pup tent."

"They hauled the body away yet?" Loving asked.

"No."

"They're saving it for you," Zenith said, and smiled; there was doughnut glaze on his face.

Hassell asked, "The local police chief . . . what's his name? Mike Nesmith? Mickey Dolenz?"

"Davey James," Dallas said, allowing himself a smile.

"Yeah, yeah—so has Peter Tork narrowed down the suspect list any?"

"Oh sure," Dallas said. "The population of Shenandoah,

six thousand, plus ten thousand bike-riders."

An ominous silence filled the patrol car—silence but for Zenith's chewing.

"Trooper Zenith," Dallas said, "I have an assignment for you."

A last fragment of doughnut between thumb and middle fingertip, Zenith shrugged. "Don't I already have an assignment? Don't we all?"

"This murder shakes all that up. You're to stay behind today and however many more days are necessary to canvass this community properly . You'll be detailed to work with the Shenandoah P.D."

"Where do I start?"

"Door to door in the neighborhood surrounding the park, and take it from there. Report in by cell phone whenever you have anything resembling a lead."

Zenith, chewing, shrugged again, saying, "Yes, sir," indifferently.

But Dallas knew Bill Zenith—seasoned trooper that he was—would do a thorough, no-nonsense job.

"Trooper Loving," Dallas said, "you've done your share of bike riding, I understand."

The handsome young trooper frowned. "Yes . . . ."

"Trooper Zenith will operate on foot and/or in tandem with the local p.d. You take the patrol car and find yourself a bike. You're joining RAGBRAI."

Now Loving's eyes popped open. "What? Why . . . ?"

"I have severe doubts the governor will shut this event

down, and the backers of RAGBRAI won't either. That means we'll have ten thousand suspects on wheels. You'll be the undercover cop among them—keeping an eye out, surreptitiously, discretely, investigating."

Thinking about that, Loving nodded, saying, "I hope I can keep up."

"It's not a race, Lars. Just join in the fun—the booths, and restaurants and taverns along the way, the nighttime festivities. Seek out those who had contact with the murder victim."

"Does he have a name?"

"Not yet. But you can bet the D.C.I. will get it for us. Go, you two."

The young cop and the older one got out of the backseat, Loving heading toward the patrol car, Zenith back into the convenience store for another doughnut.

And Dallas, coffee cup drained, feeling alive finally, turned the engine back on and headed for the little park and the big murder.

The police chief, Davey James, was a career cop of fifty-plus years, but he might have been just another RAGBRAI participant in his plaid shirt and khaki trousers. Tanned, graying, beefy, James ushered Dallas and Hassell to the burnt pup tent. The corpse was a black slab of timber, only its general shape making it discernible as human. The pearl-handled switchblades—one in either eye—were like bizarre markers, little flag poles robbed of their pennants.

"The D.C.I. mobile lab should be here soon," Dallas told the chief. Hassell was combing the area, moving slowly in an ever-expanding circle, around the death site.

James' uniformed men—half a dozen of them (the whole department? Dallas wondered)—had this section of the park cordoned off. But the crowd of RAGBRAI bikers milled just beyond, faces pale with fright and concern and curiosity. Though the sky was just beginning to turn the faded blue of coming dawn, no one was sleeping; RAGBRAI's second day was getting off to an unusual start.

"We just got word," James said. "The event goes on."

"But you're holding everyone for now, right?" Dallas said, with a frown. "You haven't released anyone, have you?"

"No. Not many complaints, either. The word has spread about this little episode. A few who like to set out early and finish the day the same, they've been bitching. But RAGBRAI's a peculiar animal—pretty laid back, generally." Then, not realizing he was echoing Dallas's own comments to his men, the chief said, "I mean, it's not a race."

Dallas glanced toward the crowd beyond the police cordon. "Well, we can't interview thousands of people without this event being postponed—and that doesn't seem to be an option."

The chief scratched his head. "What do you propose, lieutenant?"

"Have your men round up anyone seen talking to our murder victim, or who might have information to volunteer. By eight o'clock you can send everybody on. We'll do more interviews tonight, at the next stop."

"All right. You don't seem happy about this, Lieutenant."

"No. A murder case with 16,000 suspects is tough enough—let alone in the context of a cross-state bike marathon. Now—let me talk to this mystery writer."

"Sure. He's been cooperative."

"He better stay that way." Dallas twitched a smile. "After all, he's our best suspect."

BARBARA COLLINS *has published some twenty short stories in such anthologies as* Lethal Ladies *(which she co-edited)*, Hot Blood, Love Kills, Marilyn: Shades of Blonde, Women on the Edge, Vengeance is Hers, Murder for Mother, Murder for Father, Murder Most Delicious, Celebrity Vampires, White House Horrors *and* Night Screams. *Her stories have appeared in most entries of the bestselling anthology series* Cat Crimes, *and several of her works have been chosen for the* Years's 25 Finest Crime and Mystery Stories *collections. She has published several stories in collaboration with her writer husband, Max Allan Collins, and their first collaborative novel,* Regeneration *(from one of their short stories), was published in October 1999. A second novel,* Bombshell, *has been sold to St. Martin's Press, and a third is in the works.*

Barbara also works as production manager on her husband's independent film projects. She and Max live in Muscatine with their teenage son, Nathan.

4
Crispy Critter

BY WENDI LEE

Trooper Zenith and Chief James were both on the scene
when the state medical examiner, George Hathaway, arrived
in Shenandoah at 7:30 in the morning. Zenith supposed
the police chief didn't like having his authority stepped on.
Besides, James did have to show Hathaway where he could
examine the body. Zenith had worked with Dr. Hathaway a
few times before and had found him to be professional with
a dry wit. Okay, not necessarily a dry wit—more like a practical joker.

The day was already muggy, Zenith noted, and the riders
were restless. Some of the participants were checking and
rechecking their supplies; others were tuning up their bicycles or had gone for a walk to get rid of the tension that
hovered in the air.

Dallas had told Zenith he and Lt. Hassel would be pulling out with the riders soon, but first they wanted to talk to
the main witnesses, the mystery writer and maybe one or

two others, and they were waiting to find out the name of the victim. One of the officials was looking up the roster to give them at least a name to go on.

"Okay, where's the crispy critter?" Dr. Hathaway asked in a loud voice. Hathaway looked like he was right out of high school, but was really in his mid-thirties. He recognized Zenith, and grinned. Zenith nodded back amiably. Dr. Hathaway strode up to Zenith.

"Where's the body? I hear he's a little on the done side."

Chief James frowned at this casual reference to the body.

"Chief James, this is Dr. Hathaway, the state medical examiner. We need a place to examine the body."

The chief's brow cleared. "Oh. Yeah, I heard you guys have a weird sense of humor. One of our doctors has offered to lend his office for your examination."

Hathaway nodded brusquely. "Lead the way, James."

A team of troopers had loaded the body into a local funeral parlor's hearse and transported the remains to the office where it waited to be examined. Dr. Hathaway wasted no time in prepping for the autopsy.

Zenith intended to leave as soon as he'd made certain the examiner had everything he needed. The trooper was used to bodies, but he didn't like to be around them any more than he had to. Besides, Lt. Dallas had asked him to be there for the interview with the mystery writer.

He was glad he didn't have Lar's job, biking across the state. He'd probably have a heart attack before he got to the next town. Zenith didn't believe in exercise as strenuous as cycling. A walk by the river was closer to his idea of stretching his muscles. And if he had a cool beer in one hand, even better.

Hathaway tossed a pair of thin rubber gloves to Zenith. "You can help me with some of the details."

Zenith glanced around and noticed that Chief James had popped his head in the door. The chief looked apologetic. "I'll wait out in the hall." He looked briefly at the charred slab on the table and shuddered.

Hathaway shrugged. "No skin off my nose." He turned his attention to the cadaver. "Speaking of skin, there's not much left of his. What kind of fire was it?"

"We think kerosene. The fire chief is looking into it at the moment, but it sure smelled like kerosene to me." Zenith glanced at his watch to avoid looking at Hathaway's examination of the two pearl-handled knives. He didn't look away quickly enough, though. His eyes just caught Hathaway wiggling the knives around experimentally. "Look, Doc, Lt. Dallas wants me over there for one of the interviews. Can you do without me?"

Hathaway leaned over the corpse and sniffed. "Kerosene's what I thought, too. Burns fast and clean. Listen. Get that other guy in here—the chief. I do need help." The medical examiner looked serious for once.

Zenith slipped out of the room, glad to be away from the sight of Hathaway pulling the knives out of the corpse's eye sockets. "Hey, Chief, can you come in here for a moment?" Chief James had his back to Zenith, and when he turned around, the trooper noticed how pale the tanned older man was. He was struggling to keep his breakfast down. James must have noticed Zenith's look, for he smiled. "I'm afraid I've never seen anything like this in all my years on the force."

Zenith raised his eyebrows. "You never had a crispy critter before?"

The chief shook his head. "I can stand blood and guts— I've seen gunshot wounds before. I've even pulled floaters out of the river."

"Nasty things, floaters," Zenith replied conversationally. James nodded.

"Look, you don't have to go in there. Hathaway's a bit of a practical joker. He's probably going to ask you to put a foot on the corpse to hold it down while he pulls the knives out or something like that. It's a way for him to relieve the stress he's under. I'll go back in." He turned to go.

The chief acted swiftly. "No, no. That's all right. I overheard Lt. Dallas telling you to get back to the interviews. Someone's gotta stay here."

"You sure?"

The chief nodded and swallowed. "I can handle it."

"I'll send over one of your men, if you'd prefer."

"Tell my second in charge, Deputy Reynolds, to get himself over here pronto." The chief opened the door and stepped inside. Zenith could hear the sound of the examiner's saw starting up as he left the building. It was faint, but he could have sworn he heard a thud, like a body hitting the floor, as well.

Lt. Dallas had set up headquarters at the sheriff's office in their only interrogation room. It was freshly painted an institutional green and had a cracked formica table with three warped metal and vinyl chairs. The interrogation room also served as the break room; a coffee machine with a pot of cold caffeine sat on a counter next to a sink. A small refrigerator hummed merrily next to the coffee machine.

Dallas and Hassell sat with a balding middle-aged man with glasses. He had a small paunch, but otherwise was in pretty good shape.

"This is Trooper Bill Zenith," Dallas told the man, then turned to Zenith. "This is Jim Wade. He was the first witness on the scene."

Dallas turned back to Wade. "Tell us what happened in your own words."

"Starting when?"

"When you met the victim. What was your impression of him?"

Wade clasped his hands together on the table. "He was a pain in the ass."

There were glances all around among the troopers. "Did this pain in the ass have a name?" Hassell asked.

"Eyepatch." Wade looked up. "I just called him Eyepatch because he wore one. He was always complaining. The food wasn't good enough, the sun was too hot, and the water wasn't cold enough. Nothing seemed to make him happier than making everyone else around him miserable."

"Why didn't you ask him his name?" Zenith asked.

Wade was looking from one trooper to the other, but he didn't look the least bit nervous. He shrugged. "He hooked up with me for some odd reason, and kept up his litany of complaints. Maybe it was because I was the only one who would let him vent, or maybe it was because he was sweet on this woman I've just met." He leaned back and folded his arms across his chest, stretching his legs out and pushing his chair back a bit at the same time.

Zenith didn't get any bad feelings about this mystery writer, but he had been known to be wrong before.

Lt. Dallas interrupted his thoughts. "Tell us about last night. Everything that happened."

Wade adjusted his glasses. "Well, let's see. I had my dinner with about nineteen other riders. We were all pretty quiet, but it had been a good day of riding and you get this camaraderie, you know?" He looked directly at Zenith, who did the only thing he could have done: he nodded, even though he didn't know.

"Tell us about this woman," Hassell prompted.

Wade nodded. "Her name is Jennie, and she likes me. And I like her. So we were talking, getting along just fine together when Eyepatch barges in."

"Did Eyepatch, as you call him, show any interest in her other than hanging around you and making a nuisance of himself?"

Wade screwed his face up as if in thought. "Not really. In fact, he didn't seem interested in anything other than spoiling other people's moods."

"How so?" Zenith asked.

"He complained about the pop not being cold enough. He wondered if they'd ever heard of cold pop in this state." Wade had the grace to look embarrassed. "I didn't pay much attention to him, but it didn't matter. He kept up the patter, switching to the hamburgers and how he'd probably get food poisoning from eating them."

He didn't have time for food poisoning, Zenith thought.

"This is when my lady friend stepped in and told him he didn't seem to behaving a very good time. Then she made a joke, and she and I left the table to go for a walk."

"I guess I find it a little hard to believe you didn't even ask him his name, yet he hung around you," Dallas said. He was rolling a pen around between his fingers.

Wade looked a little uncomfortable. "I didn't ask his name because . . . . " His hesitation made Zenith lean forward.

"Go on," Hassell urged.

"Well, I saw the knives once before. They fell out of his backpack earlier in the day. He knew I'd seen the knives. I made a joke out of it. He didn't think it was funny. That bothered me. Made me think this guy was looking for trouble. I didn't want to be the one who gave it to him."

"Why didn't you say anything to the officials?"

Wade took his glasses off and rubbed the bridge of his nose. "I didn't get a chance. It was something I was thinking of doing. But like I said before, I didn't want to be the one who gave him trouble."

There wasn't much more to ask Jim Wade. Lt. Dallas told

the writer he could go, but to stay with RAGBRAI where they could get in touch with him if he was needed.

Zenith accompanied the writer out of the station.

"Thanks for coming in," Zenith said. "What kind of mysteries do you write?"

Wade flashed a smile, clearly relieved to be talking about something else. "Oh, thrillers and suspense. I'm what the publishing industry calls a mid-list writer. I fill out the catalog around luminaries like Stephen King and Tom Clancy."

"But you make a living from it," Zenith said. "You must enjoy your work."

Wade took off his glasses and polished the lenses. "I do, but my ex-wife hated what I do for a living."

"Ah, a free man."

Wade allowed himself a short laugh. "You might say that, but I'm finding that being single and dating again is a whole different animal from when I was in my twenties."

"You're not doing so bad." Zenith nodded in the direction of a lovely woman, probably in her early forties, who seemed to be waiting for the writer. She was medium height, had firm thighs, a trim waist, and wore her brown wavy hair pulled back into a loose ponytail. At the moment, she had a worried expression that tightened the corners of her eyes, but Zenith bet himself that when she was happy, her smile lit up a room. "That the woman who talked to Eyepatch?"

Wade grinned. "Guess I'm doing okay. Yeah, that's Jennie Wyman. She's very" he hesitated, then finished his thought, "nice. Jennie is a very nice woman."

"I hope things go well for you two. Why don't you tell her to stick around. We'll be wanting to talk to her in a minute."

Wade nodded and walked away. Zenith retreated into the station. One of the deputies, a young man who looked like he'd recently graduated from high school, approached him. "You're one of the troopers?"

Zenith nodded.

"We just got in an identification on the victim. His name is Tom Spurgeon." The deputy handed Zenith a paper with all the pertinent information.

Zenith brought the report back into the interrogation room where Lars Loving had joined Dallas and Hassel.

"Nice shorts," Zenith said as he eyed his partner's lime green bike shorts with the yellow stripe down the sides, a yellow shirt clinging to his weightlifter's chest. "Oh, yeah, you'll blend right in."

Dallas and Hassel were trying to keep straight faces.

Loving's face turned bright red. "It was all they had left in the store."

Zenith turned to Dallas. "The report is in."

"Tell us about the victim."

Zenith read the information off the sheet. "Thomas Michael Spurgeon, forty-seven years old, six feet, one-ninety-eight. Lived in Joliet, was a prison guard until he up and quit, moved to Waterloo, and opened a gun shop. Divorced. Reasonable good health."

"Until recently," Dallas thought. "Any arrest record?"

Zenith scanned the next page. "Spurgeon had been

arrested several times for domestic violence in Joliet, but nothing since September of 1997."

"Probably when he got a divorce," Loving said.

"Here's something," Zenith said. "Why would someone wear an eyepatch in a bicycle ride across Iowa when he had two good eyes?"

WENDI LEE *is the author of ten books, including a PI series featuring Boston-born ex-marine Angela Matelli. Published by St. Martin's Press, the third and latest book is called* Deadbeat. *The fourth installment,* The Man with the Most Toys Dies, *will be released later this year. Lee is currently working on the fifth Angela Matelli mystery, tentatively titled* Voodoo U.

5

A Quarter-note Breeze

By Kurt Ullrich

Late on that long green July morning 70-year-old Ruby Goodnight sat in a wicker chair on her front porch on Elm Street in Shenendoah, drinking lemonade, thinking about her town, a town she knew well.

Ruby was well-known in southwest Iowa. For decades she was an overworked, underpaid, well-respected reporter for *Valley News Today*, a newspaper which covered Shenandoah, Red Oak, and Clarinda. Ruby could tell you about any local events dating back to the 1950s, when the paper was called the *Evening Standard*. She retired from the newspaper business a couple of years ago, but still kept close tabs on the local news. The police scanner on her nightstand squawked day and night.

At the time of her retirement she and the new publisher were feuding about the trend toward knocking down the figurative wall between the advertising department and the news department. She felt that to do so was to compromise everything journalism was about. The young publisher thought Ruby was obstinate and old-fashioned. She felt he was irresponsible and dim-witted. Not to mention the fact that he was a lot more concerned about his perfect hair, his golf game, and his Rotary and Chamber memberships than about anything resembling journalism.

The last straw for her was when he insisted that she ditch her spiral-bound "Reporter's Notebook" and start hauling around a laptop computer. She knew then that the rational world was losing its grip, so she retired.

Ruby had hoped to spend her remaining years writing a book or two. She had begun one about some long-ago axe murders which took place in nearby Villisca, but she couldn't sustain her interest. She wanted something more immediate. Now she was working on a book about a more recent murder of a farmer near Farragut.

She and her constant companion, a small black and white cat named Lawrence, spent as much time as possible sitting on the front porch of her bungalow near Priest Park, reading Dickens and Grisham. Lawrence did more napping than reading, something Ruby also found herself doing more often than she cared to admit. And she thought about her town. Shenandoah was one of those towns where, if you're lucky, you'll arrive in the summer at sunset, when the town is bathed in golden, slanted light. It's a neat, charming town; a bit of Frank Capra's Bedford Falls mixed in with Thornton Wilder's Grover's Corners. A perfect place to call home. Even

Ruby's elm-less Elm Street was right out of a Norman Rockwell dream.

And one of the best things about Shenandoah is Ruby Goodnight. She has the face and demeanor of a thousand carefree summers. To see Ruby's face is to experience that day in the spring when the windows are flung open for the first time since last autumn, and summer drifts musically in on a quarter-note breeze, smelling of sweet lilacs and youthful expectation.

Ruby was engrossed in the latest fiction by Frank Conroy while Lawrence kept an eye on the swallows wheeling around the neighborhood when a uniformed state trooper stepped up onto her porch. He sounded like someone climbing onto an old saddle, leather creaking with each move. She had been expecting him.

"Good morning!" he said, smiling. "I'm Officer Bill Zenith and everyone I've met in town so far has told me that if I've got questions I need to go see Ruby, because she knows everything. Are you Ruby Goodnight?"

"Yes," Ruby said, smiling back at the congenial officer. "Come on up. Let me move Lawrence from the chair; he won't mind. I don't know much about your dead bicyclist, if that's why you're here."

Zenith's jaw dropped ever-so-slightly. "How do you know about it at all? We've tried to keep this sort of quiet, at least until we've had a chance to interview some people."

Ruby looked amused, saying, "How does one know anything in a small town? Word travels fast, and sometimes it's even accurate. Besides, Chief James gets on that radio of his and, before you know it, everybody in a 30-mile radius knows about it. Heck, I can tell you which married men are messing with the morning shift waitress down at the Depot Restaurant just by listening to the guys on their radios."

Smiling, nodding, and turning a little red, Zenith began asking the usual police canvassing questions. She wasn't able to provide much help, but she made a statement which took him by surprise. "I heard Chief James say something interesting," she said. "Something about a switchblade in each eye. That's a pretty strong message for a murderer to send, but not unheard of around here."

"What do you mean?" Zenith asked.

"Well, a couple of years ago a farmer down by Farragut was murdered in his barn and the murderer, who was never found, left a knife in each of the victim's eyes. The farmer's name was Carey. After the murder the barn was set on fire. It was pretty gruesome. I covered the story for the local papers and even gave a couple of stories to the folks at the *Register* in Des Moines. During the initial investigation I got to know a D.C.I. agent who told me there is a serial killer loose in the Midwest who likes to leave cutlery in the eyes of his victims."

"Is there anything else?" asked Zenith.

"Yes, there is. I was talking to my neighbor, Paul Ingram, this morning. He works over at Hackett-Livingston Funeral

Home and he was the one who picked up the body at the park to deliver it to the local medical clinic. He's no doctor, but he's seen a lot of dead bodies, and he noticed what he thought were additional stab wounds in the body and thought that perhaps the victim was dead before the switchblades were shoved into the eyes. I understand that some medical examiner type named Hathaway is coming down to look at the body. I don't know where he's from; Iowa hasn't quite figured out how to hire and keep medical examiners; he's probably from Nebraska."

She turned a little, watching Lawrence stalk a ground squirrel, and continued, "I've known a few medical examiners over the years. A different sort altogether. The science of what they do is secondary to the drama of the whole thing. You know, police, F.B.I., D.C.I., yellow police tape, flashing lights, sirens, and the media."

Ruby went on, "Me, I find death very frightening. It scares me terribly. I thought that as I got older I'd learn to welcome death, that there would be an ever-deepening tiredness that would come over me. But I've seen death too many times to know that's not how it works. It's usually unexpected and full of pain. I want death to be a quiet invitation to slumber in cool, snow-white sheets on a day like today, easy, relaxed, and right. It scares me to know that death will undoubtedly be something I cannot control. That frightens me, and makes me a little sad, sad knowing that this glorious world will go on without me."

Ruby Goodnight was somewhere else, traveling across

landscapes far from Shenandoah, light years away from this trooper sitting with her on a summer porch. Her thoughtful green eyes adjusted themselves to a different light and he knew she was in a world of her own, a sweet place where he couldn't follow her. He sat quietly and waited for this woman, who was old enough to be his mother, to return to him.

As he looked at the soft, gentle face of Ruby Goodnight he thought about what an interesting woman she seemed to be, interesting in the way that people are who have been through a lot and come out on the other side intact. Turning toward him, looking a little surprised, she said, "Sorry, I got off the track for a bit. Excuse an old lady for thinking out loud."

"Quite all right; I rather enjoyed it."

"I baked some chocolate chip cookies last night. Might I interest you in any?" she asked.

Never one to turn down an offer of food, Zenith gladly accepted, saying, "Yes, thank you. That would be nice. Let me make a quick call to my boss and I'll be right back."

He walked to his patrol cruiser and called Lt. Dallas on the radio. "Scott, Bill here. Hey, listen. I just heard we might be talkin' serial killer and that the victim might have already been dead when the knives were jammed into his eyes. Is this true? You knew about it?"

Zenith started to burn. "Goddamit, Scott, how come I hear this from a little old lady and not you? It's bad enough that the D.C.I. thinks all we're capable of is writing speeding tickets, and then you send me out to investigate with only partial information! Geez this is irritating. All right, all right, apologies accepted. Is there anything else you haven't told me? Good, I'll talk to you later."

As he walked back up the sidewalk toward the porch he wondered if any of this was worth it. He was dealing with idiots. He'd always wanted to be a teacher; maybe it wasn't too late.

This is a peaceful town, he thought. Maybe he'd get his teaching certificate and move to Shenandoah. In the distance he could hear a train crossing the prairie, carrying freight toward Omaha. A couple of doors down children were playing catch with a ball in the front yard.

As he walked he noticed Ruby Goodnight's hollyhocks, sweet william, and forget-me-nots. With each step he felt more mellow and less like a cop. He felt the soothing balm of shimmering heat on this lazy July morning. For a little while his investigation could wait. It was going to be a long week and, thinking of cookies and all things good, he gave Ruby Goodnight a huge smile, joining her on the porch.

KURT A. ULLRICH's *essays appear regularly in the* Des Moines Register, Quad-City Times, *and* Chicago Tribune. *He and his wife, Iowa District Court Judge Bobbi M. Alpers, live in rural Jackson County on Whisper Hollow Farm.*

6

Jim Wade
and the Marvelaires

By Vince Gotera

I was sure sweating. Sweating rivulets, as a lazy mystery writer might say. Or sweating bullets. Or just plain sweating. It wasn't all that hot on this second day, maybe 85 degrees. But it could have been a hundred in the shade the way I felt. I kept thinking about that young man sixteen years ago who had had a heart attack somewhere on this stretch of road, the first RAGBRAI fatality.

Jennie and I had pedaled out of Shenandoah sometime around nine, part of a long line of RAGBRAI riders, color and flash. Jennie was quiet. Didn't want to talk about being questioned by the state troopers, maybe.

We pedaled in silence for a while. Pretty soon, though, I was being silent myself because I was huffing and puffing. Especially on some of those hills. Rolling hills. I felt like we had been dropped—kerplunk—right in the middle of a Grant

Wood painting. Spherical trees, big round hills. Pretty, but tough for biking.

We stopped for lemonade in Essex and kicked back a bit. Just sitting on a bench and watching riders go by. Jennie sure looked pretty. She wore a magenta shirt-and-shorts outfit. Quite fetching actually.

Earlier, on some of the tougher hills she had ridden ahead, maybe to give a middle-aged guy like me some privacy as I struggled, my teeth dry with dust. But even under those circumstances, I would look ahead now and then to where she was standing up on her pedals, marveling at the wonderful view. Sitting on that bench and thinking back to her up on the pedals, I tried hard not to say anything politically incorrect.

So anyway, there we were, sipping lemonade, enjoying the slight breeze, when a muscle-bound guy in a godawful lime-green and lemon-yellow ensemble slowed and then swung back toward us. I remember thinking to myself with a chuckle that he looked like a walking billboard for a soft drink—you know, lemon-lime—and then it occurred to me that with those broad shoulders and barrel chest he appeared to be some kind of superhero. Especially with that bright stripe going down the side of his skin-tight leotard shorts.

"Hey, Jennie! Howzit going?" Lemon-lime squinted down at us on our bench.

"Lars!" Jennie laughed. "What are you doing here? Are you investigating that murder?"

"Pretty strange, huh." He smiled, though it seemed

unconvincing to me as a smile. "No, I'm on vacation this week. Just here for the fun of it."

Jennie turned to me with a bright twinkle in her eye. "Jim, this is Lars. He's a state trooper. Lars, Jim. Mystery writer and published author. Oh, sorry: Jim Wade, Lars Loving."

"Hi, Lars." I got up and shook his hand. We both squeezed too tight. Lars Loving. Hmm. Double L's, like Lana Lang, Lex Luthor, Lois Lane, Lemon Lime.

As the three of us got back on the road, Jennie filled me in—how she had met Lars in a criminology class at the University of Northern Iowa. She had really enjoyed that class, taught by Ed Epperly, a visiting professor from Luther College. She and Lars were old friends, she said. Nothing more.

As we neared Bethesda, we pulled up at a picturesque Lutheran Church. Quite a sight greeted us. There was a reporter for the *Des Moines Register* interviewing some costumed RAGBRAI types. Later we found out the reporter's name was Charlie Andropoulos and she was looking for RAGBRAI color.

Well, she had sure found it. A lot of color. Charlie was standing in the shade of that church with four guys. The one she was talking to as we rode up was really fit, well built, maybe around forty years old. The weird thing was that he had on a skin-tight blue suit with bright red gloves and boots like a musketeer and vertical red and white stripes around his midriff. The suit blended into a tight hood over his head with little white wings flaring out over his ears. On the forehead of the hood was a white star and his chest was emblazoned with a white letter A. He was carrying a round shield, red, white and blue, with a white star in the middle.

The guy next to him was dressed in even stranger fashion. He had on heavy black tights. (Boy, I didn't envy him that costume on this hot day.) A dark blue, velvety tunic was belted with a golden sash. When he turned towards me I saw that on the chest the tunic was embroidered with a light blue shape, like a bird soaring upward toward a large round medallion, like a golden amulet. He was wearing a red cape edged in yellow filigree. His head was equally striking: stark black hair with blazes of white stretching back from the temples.

The third guy was a Herculean fellow, much larger than Lars, with shoulder-length blond hair held back by a silver helmet with bright wings arching up and back. He had been poured into a sleeveless outfit, and he wore gold wristbands and leather straps around his leggings. Because he too had on a cape, I couldn't see too well what was tucked into his belt—some kind of hammer, maybe. Man, this was pretty strange.

The fourth guy's outfit was immediately recognizable and seeing him clued me in right away. He was completely covered from head to foot in spandex, red hood, red shoulders, red gloves, red boots, with the rest of his body in blue. All over the suit were black lines like spiderwebs. And on his chest and upper back was his logo, a black one on the front and a red one in back: spiders.

Yep, it was Spider-Man. And the other three were Captain America, Doctor Strange, and Thor. Now there was a bike team! Jennie and I—and Lars—stood and gawked as did several other riders. The four superheroes were drawing a crowd.

"Yeah, we've been together for over twenty, going on thirty years." Captain America was answering one of Charlie's questions. "In the late 70s, we were hired as a group to be a bike team in the movie *Breaking Away*. It's really hard to pick us out of the crowd on the screen, but we've been a bike team since. We're all from Iowa, from this area. Thor here is from Villisca, and the rest of us are from Red Oak, Nodaway, Hepburn—all born and raised on farms."

He swept an arm with a sweeping gesture around the horizon. All of us who were watching turned our heads in synch with his motion as if he were pointing out a deer running along a distant ridge.

"Have you been in other races then? *Breaking Away* was quite a while ago." Charlie pulled the interview back on task as she flipped a page in her small notebook.

"Oh, yeah." Thor picked up the narrative. "We've been in races all over the country. All kinds of races. Triathlons. Even marathons, so no bikes. In 1985, we ran the Bay-to-Breakers Race in San Francisco. That was the toughest seven miles I ever did on foot. Talk about hills. You start at one side of the city, on the Bay, and run to the other side of the city, the Pacific Ocean."

"That race is renowned for crazy costumes. Isn't that right?"

Charlie licked the tip of her pencil.

"Definitely. That was the first time we raced in costume." Thor drew himself up, as if proudly. "We went as the X-men that time. Another year, we ran the Bay-to-Breakers as the incredible Hulk. Four incredible Hulks. Can you imagine that? All of us in green face and body makeup, wearing purple jeans—cutoffs."

Charlie raised an eyebrow. "Why those particular costumes?"

It was Doctor Strange's turn. "Because they're all comic-book characters." He almost seemed snippy, like he was going to call her a name. "When we were kids we used to read comic books together at each other's houses. All of us really wanted to get out of here then. And we loved Marvel comics. We used to call ourselves the Marvelaires—"

"Eight years ago, we rode in a kinetic sculpture race in northern California," Spider-Man interrupted. "You had to build a contraption that could move on asphalt, mud, sand, whatever, but it also had to float. We were the Fantastic Four. I was Johnny Storm, or the Human Torch. Cap there was Reed Richards, Mr. Fantastic. Thor, since he's so big, played Ben Grimm, the Thing. We glued orange sponges all over his body. And Doc here, since he's the shortest, played Sue Richards, the Invisible Girl."

Doctor Strange seemed to be scowling just a bit.

Spidey continued, "We built a Fantastic Four gizmo space-ship out of PVC, with the four of us on bikes inside, waving to people through plexiglass. With all that closed-up pipe and a few strategic pontoons, we floated pretty good when we crossed Humboldt Bay."

"I notice you keep referring to each other by your character names." Charlie looked around at each of their faces. "What are your real names?"

"Oh, we can't tell you that." Cap again. "We're wanted by the law." All four of them laughed, rather mirthlessly. "Okay, that's it! We need to get back on the road."

As Charlie packed her notes into her backpack, and as riders who had stopped to watch began taking off, I said to Jennie, "That was pretty weird."

"You mean the costumes?"

"No, the way they all laughed at the end. Something creepy about it. They laughed, but it didn't seem like laughing." I got back on my bike.

"I know what you mean," Lars was stroking his chin. "I seem to remember hearing something about a murder that took place at the same time and in the same place as that kinetic sculpture race."

The four superheroes were on their bikes by this time, and we all took off together. I rode with Captain America until we reached Hepburn and we talked about this and that. Then we headed east to US 71 and headed for Villisca. The ride eased up as we got closer. The hills leveled out as we reached the rise where Villisca is situated.

We stopped at the town square in Villisca and were served bacon and eggs—even though it was the middle of the afternoon. This town wants to be known as the "bacon and egg" capital of Iowa since it has a state-of-the-art egg-laying facility and there are livestock farms in the vicinity, but it is most well known for a notorious unsolved crime, the Villisca axe murders of 1912, when an entire family and two neighbor girls sleeping over were bludgeoned to death.

After eating, the Marvelaires invited us to see something with them. "This is like a pilgrimage for us," Thor said, leading the way.

We walked west off the town square. In the middle of the block ahead of us was City Hall, a former bank building from the look of it, flanked by storefronts on either side. It was a weathered gray stone building, two stories with a kind of flat Greek portico look. We entered through a glass door and then through some older swinging doors inside. Thor led us to a display case in the lobby.

Here was the Villisca axe itself. An ordinary looking axe, with a single bit. Probably three feet long. You could have bought an axe like it in probably any hardware store. There was a distinctive detail to it, though, and that was a two-inch cylindrical knob lathed into the tail end of the shaft. The cylinder was a little wider than the main shaft so it probably served as a kind of brace for the hand.

Thor then reached for his hammer. He held it next to the axe in the case. I was wrong. He didn't have a stone sledgehammer like Thor in the Marvel comic books. This was an exact replica of the Villisca axe. Exact, down to the India-ink markings on the original Roman numerals placed there during the original court case to indicate exhibit numbers.

"The axe is blunt," Thor said in a rather loud stage whisper. "Josiah Moore—he was the father of the family killed—Josiah only used it to break up coal. He didn't need it to be sharp because he never chopped wood with it. It's four pounds, six ounces."

I shuddered a little, thinking of that family and the blunt axe.

We went back out on the square. Thor swung his axe in great circles around his head. I thought it was all a little weird. "How come you know so much about the murders?"

Cap said, "Thor was born and raised here."

I wasn't convinced. I bet lots of folks in Villisca don't carry around replicas of notorious murder weapons.

Thor hooked the axe back into his belt. "You know they never solved the case." He looked around as if to make sure we were all looking at him. "The original theory was that there was a serial killer. In 1904, there was a series of murders, first in Colorado, then Illinois, then Kansas, all on subsequent weekends, with entire families killed. No one was ever caught. Then eight years later, there was another murder in Kansas the Wednesday before the murders here, which took place on a Sunday.

"Nope, they never solved it. Some people said it was Frank Jones, a state senator who had been a bitter competitor of Josiah Moore's, his former boss. Moore had been sleeping with Jones's daughter-in-law—that was the scuttlebutt. A detective named Wilkerson tied Senator Jones to William

'Blackie' Mansfield, a guy from Illinois whose wife, daughter, and in-laws had been murdered with an axe. Supposedly Jones had hired Blackie to kill the Moores. But Blackie got off because it was proven that a boarder had done the murders in Illinois.

"Then they indicted a Reverend Kelly. He was quite the pervert, it seemed, a real loony. He confessed twice to killing the Moores and then recanted. He got off too. See, you *can* get away with a perfect crime. We still don't know who did it." Thor shook his head, seemingly in admiration at the inexplicability of it all.

At that point, we all mounted our bikes and rode off. It was truly strange to ride past the Moore house; I guess the RAGBRAI folks wanted to route us past the house because it was famous.

But Thor's little story had put a chill on our talk, and the five-hour ride to Creston was silent and uneventful. Both Jennie and Lars were quiet the whole way. I kept thinking about Thor swinging that axe outside the Villisca City Hall.

After we reached Creston and put up our tents, Jennie and I took a walk after dinner near the little lake in McKinley Park, one of three RAGBRAI campsites in Creston. It was simply beautiful. The sun was going down and there was an unbelievable tinge of purple shading to a pinkish orange in the western sky. Jennie and I held hands.

Lars went to the rock concert at Southwestern Community College that night, where the band Doomsday Refreshment Committee was performing, but Jennie and I skipped it. Too tired, I guess. After Jennie had retired to her tent, Captain America came over and said he wanted to show me something. He led me towards a large oak tree away from the other campsites. It wasn't full dark yet.

"Do you like knives?" he said.

Like a gunfighter from the old west, Cap suddenly had butterfly knives in both hands, and he spun them open simultaneously. Locking them with a deft twist of his wrists, he flipped them in the air so that he was gripping each knife by the blade. Quite an impressive performance, like a deadly kind of juggling. He threw both knives at the same time toward the tree and they lodged, vibrating, as if the tree had suddenly acquired two eyes.

"You know, Cap," I said. "I noticed you've got the A on your chest. In the old comic books, Captain America's A was on his head."

"Yeah, I took some liberties with the costume. I couldn't resist having it be like the scarlet letter."

"Really? But why? What does the letter mean to you?"

There was an ominous pause before Cap's reply.

"Avenger."

VINCE GOTERA *teaches multicultural literature and creative writing at the University of Northern Iowa. He has published two books,* Dragonfly *(a collection of poems) and* Radical Visions *(a critical study of poetry written by Vietnam veterans). His short stories may be found in* Fiction by Filipinos in America *and* Tilting the Continent: Southeast Asian American Literature *(forthcoming).*

Vince was born and raised in San Francisco, although he also lived for some time as a child in the Philippines. He resides in Cedar Falls with his wife, Mary Ann, and their four children, Amanda, Amelia, Melina, and Gabriel. He also has a grown-up son, Marty, who lives in San Francisco. Vince plays bass guitar in the band Rock of Ages.

7

"The Big Story"

By Amy Johnson

It was one of the biggest stories of the year. Perhaps the biggest story of my career. But if you had told me that the highlight of my twelve-year odyssey in broadcast journalism would be RAGBRAI XXVIII, I would have laughed out loud.

Not that RAGBRAI isn't near and dear to my heart. My name is Kristen Jensen. Before becoming a correspondent for NBC's *Today Show*, I cut my teeth as a young reporter at KWWL, the NBC affiliate in Waterloo, Iowa. In 1990, one of my first traveling assignments was to cover RAGBRAI XVIII, a scenic 495-mile journey from Sioux Center to Burlington. I rode every mile that year, charmed by the beauty of the Iowa countryside and its residents. I remember the sight of dew on the corn first thing in the morning, and the hum of locusts in the air last thing at night. The sight of church steeples beckoning us in the distance, and the cool spray of water from sprinklers, welcoming us as we rode into tiny Iowa towns.

In all fairness, I also remember the utter exhaustion of "working" RAGBRAI for a small, local TV station. From sunup to long past sundown, I was a "Jill of All Trades"—an athlete, photographer, writer, and editor. When I wasn't actually peddling up the hills, I was looking at them through the viewfinder of my camera. In between, I was doing everything from hauling cable to hauling trash. On one memorable RAGBRAI afternoon in Manchester, I spent several hours sitting on an old milk can in a barn, editing my videotape for that night's story.

Soon after my fourth RAGBRAI in 1995, I was plucked out of obscurity by the charm school in the cornfield known as Frank N. Magid and Associates of Marion. They helped me land a job in New York as a correspondent for NBC. So, when my producer at my current employer—*The Today Show*—asked me if I wanted to cover RAGBRAI XXVIII, I jumped at the chance. I longed for the fresh air, open spaces, and friendly faces of the Hawkeye state. Besides, as a network reporter, I wouldn't have to go it alone. What I once used to do single-handedly as a KWWL reporter, I could now accomplish with the help of eight other people. It was going to be a fun, relaxing, and nostalgic way to spend a beautiful week in July.

Or so I thought.

So there I was on the second night of RAGBRAI: near the front lawn of the Creston Courthouse, sitting in the NBC satellite truck. Covering a murder story. By now, every member of the working press in the state—and many around the country—knew the gory details of the murder on RAGBRAI. The feeding frenzy had begun.

"It doesn't make any sense," I told NBC Producer John Richter over the phone. John was a veteran with tremendous news judgment, but the kind of personality that makes a cup of coffee nervous.

"When you think of RAGBRAI, you don't think of violent crime. Remember, John, this is the ride known around the country for its hospitality and generosity. People don't even lock up their bikes on RAGBRAI. It's the last place you'd imagine a murder would take place."

"Whatever, Kristen. This has all the makings of a ratings blockbuster. You know: a brutal murder, in the middle of nowhere, in the midst of a huge event. You literally have THOUSANDS of suspects out there! So, Kristen, I don't care if it doesn't make sense. I have NBC, MSNBC, CNBC, and every NBC affiliate in the country breathing down my neck. I just want you to go out there and get the Big Story. Better yet, find the suspect and interview him LIVE."

"OK, John. OK." I knew where this conversation was going. "But I'm going to need your help," I said. "Dig up more information on the murdered guy, Tom Spurgeon. I need details about those domestic violence charges against him. Did he do jail time? And what about that patch over his eye—and those knives he carried? Most important, why in the world was he on RAGBRAI? He certainly didn't seem like the fanny pack and toe clip type."

"I'll work on it," replied John. "And while I'm at it, I'll see if I can dig up more on the ex-wife. Maybe we can locate her and get her to talk on camera. She might be able to tell us more about old One Eye."

"John, if I'm ever going to get any work done, I have to get off the phone. I'll talk to you again in an hour or so about the live shots tonight."

"OK, Kristen. Bye"

I opened the door of the satellite truck and peered outside. It was one of those clear, calm summer nights just after dusk—the kind I used to treasure when I lived in the Hawkeye state. The pinkish-orange color of the sky had already faded to black, and stars were beginning to twinkle in the summer sky. It was all so familiar.

But yet it wasn't. This wasn't the RAGBRAI I remembered at all. That RAGBRAI was a model of civility and kindness. It was one week each year when people did nice things for each other just because they *wanted* to do them. Seven days a year when time and lines didn't seem to matter because everyone was headed in the same direction.

Now, everything was different. A murder had taken place on RAGBRAI, and a very violent murder at that. Who had done it? And how could anything like that happen here? As I watched the stars pop out of the clear, black sky, I knew that the line that once divided RAGBRAI and the rest of the world was gone. This year, the big, ugly world was riding on RAGBRAI.

I walked down the steps of the satellite truck and called out to my photographer, Justin. Together we began walking away from the courthouse toward the town square, the setting of one of two RAGBRAI parties being held in Creston that night. It was quite a sight. Thousands of bicyclists were gathered there—refreshed after a shower and a rest. On one end of the square were dozens of vendors, selling everything from lemonade and pork sandwiches to bicycle seat covers and flourescent jewelry. On the other end, hundreds of people were packed into a giant beverage garden, rocking to the tunes of Jiff and the Choosy Mothers, who played on a makeshift stage. The town of Creston was literally bursting at the seams.

Suddenly, Justin felt a tap on his shoulder, and heard a loud male voice behind him.

"Justin? Justin, is that you?"

Justin spun around and immediately started to smile. "Jim! Jim Wade!" he yelled above the roar of the band. "How the heck are you?"

"Fine," Jim hollered back. "A little worse for wear, but I'm surviving so far!"

Jim Wade? Did he say Jim Wade? Was this the same Jim Wade that Lt. Scott Dallas of the State Patrol had told me about earlier in the day? According to Lt. Dallas, a mystery writer named Jim Wade was one of the last people to see Tom Spurgeon alive in Shenandoah.

"How are things in Waverly?" Justin shouted at Jim.

"I'm still teaching now and then at Wartburg," Jim yelled

back. "And doing a little writing. Have you been back to visit your alma mater recently?"

"Excuse me," I shouted. "You're Jim Wade? Jim Wade—the mystery writer?"

"Why yes," he yelled. "Why?"

"Mr. Wade, do you mind if I speak with you a moment—away from the music?"

The three of us moved to a quieter area, a small park, only a short distance from the town square.

I was afraid someone could actually hear my heart pounding. "Mr. Wade, my name is Kristen Jensen, and I'm a correspondent for NBC. I was told by a source on the Iowa State Patrol that you were one of the last people to see Tom Spurgeon alive last night in Shenandoah."

Jim Wade looked like he'd seen a ghost.

"Was that his name?" he said. "I didn't know his name. And how do you—how do you know all this?"

"I'm sorry, Mr. Wade. I don't mean to upset you. But the media is well aware of this murder—and unfortunately, we're now also aware of you. You probably know that you're a suspect?"

Jim Wade said nothing.

"Would you like to tell your side of the story?"

"I'd really rather not," said Jim. "I haven't reached my lawyer yet—and besides, it's been a rough couple of days. I'm not really thinking clearly right now."

I glanced at Justin.

"Look, Jim, we're friends," he said. "I don't want to make

you do anything you don't want to do. But the sooner you tell your side of the story, the sooner you might be cleared as a suspect. This might actually help get you off the hook."

Jim Wade sighed heavily and looked around to see if anyone else was close by.

"OK," he said.

And that's how I got his story. An exclusive story.

For the better part of an hour, Jim Wade and I sat on those benches while Justin shot the interview. Jim told me about his career, his divorce, and the pain of being alone. He also told me how excited he was to join RAGBRAI this year, and how it made him forget his age, his ex-wife, and the rejection he had felt. In fact, he told me how thrilled he was to be 48 and have the attention of young women again.

He also told me about his brief encounter with the man he called Eyepatch. He described the man's unusual appearance, disposition, and the way the guy latched on to him and his female friend the night before. Jim described the horror of finding his body, and his confusion over a motive for the crime. He also confessed that he suddenly wasn't feeling too safe himself.

After an hour, I had everything I needed. And then some. I also had a very creepy feeling about Jim Wade. Sure, he seemed innocent enough. But as we talked, he began to invade my personal space. He kept trying to touch my arm, to inch closer to me and stare deeply into my eyes. At one point he asked how to reach me in the satellite truck, and wondered if I might be interested in having a beer later that night. It was inappropriate behavior, I thought, not to mention very odd. Afterall, I was a network reporter and he was the subject of my interview. He had just witnessed a murder. For a man who claimed to lack confidence, and expressed concern for his personal safety, Jim Wade was not "walking the walk." And it really began to bother me.

Thank God for deadlines. After glancing down at my watch, I quickly excused myself and raced back to the satellite truck. While Justin fed the interview back to New York, I called John to fill him in.

"Great," he told me. "Marcia Clark wants you to do her show on CNBC, John Gibson wants you to do his show on MSNBC, and *Dateline* wants a customized report. You also need to tape a segment tonight that Matt and Katie can use first thing in the morning."

So much for a good night's sleep.

But by 6:00 the next morning I had my bicycle gear together and was ready to go. Afterall, that was part of the deal. When NBC asked me to cover RAGBRAI, I agreed to do it under one condition: I wanted to ride every mile of every day as I had done every other year.

"There's just no way to capture the spirit of RAGBRAI," I told my producer, "unless you're on a bicycle out on the route."

And murder or no murder, today I was going to ride. After grabbing a cup of coffee at a roadside stand, I began the day's journey. Seventy-one miles of hilly, picturesque countryside from Creston to Des Moines—including a stop in Winterset, home to *The Bridges of Madison County*. Like thousands of others, I loved that book and movie, and was anxious to see where Robert Kincaid and Francesca Johnson (not to mention Clint Eastwood and Meryl Streep) played out their romance. I wanted to see the spot near the covered bridge where Robert snapped Francesca's picture; the Northside Café, where Francesca ate ice cream; and the gas station where Francesca and Robert said their final, nonverbal goodbye. OK, I know. I'm a hopeless romantic. And a really big fan.

So here I was—in the heart of the heartland—lost in the plot of *The Bridges of Madison County*. Suddenly, I heard the familiar "Boom, ba-da Boom, ba-da Boom" of Team Bad Boy. They were still a quarter mile away, but I could already feel the bass beat of their boom boxes. Behind them was Team Attitude, shouting mockingly at anyone and everyone, "GET OUT OF MY WAY! GET OUT OF MY WAY!" And behind them, The Killer Bees, whose trademark "B-Z-Z-Z-Z-Z-Z" is near-legend on RAGBRAI. By now, I was grinning from ear to ear. There's nothing like RAGBRAI.

The miles seemed to fly by. I made all the usual food pit stops: Chris Cakes for breakfast and the Pork Chop man ("PORK CHO-O-O-O-O-P-P-P-P-P-P!!!") for lunch. I was having so much fun I had almost forgotten The Big Story. Then I saw a guy ride past me with two pearl-handled switchblades driven into "eyes" drawn on his helmet. Obviously, the story was out. Leave it to a RAGBRAI rider to mock a murder.

Before long it was early afternoon, and I was in Winterset. I stood in the town square, eyeing the gas station used for Clint Eastwood's and Meryl Streep's emotional goodbye in the movie.

"Actually, it's fake," said a voice behind me.

"Excuse me?" I said.

"The gas station—it's a fake," said the woman. "It's not a working gas station. They just built the facade for the movie."

"I don't care," I responded. "If Clint Eastwood stood next to it, it's the real deal to me."

We both succumbed into giggles.

"I'm Jennie Wyman," she said, extending her hand. "And I'm Kristen Jensen," I said, extending mine.

"I take it you're a big *Bridges of Madison County* fan too?" she asked.

"Fan? Are you kidding? I'm President of the Fan Club!" I exclaimed. "I'm still searching for *my* Robert Kincaid!"

"Well, good luck," said Jennie. "Because he's the last of a dying breed."

We both started giggling again.

Jennie and I spent the better part of an hour together, getting to know each other. She told me that she lived in Cedar Falls and was a regular on RAGBRAI. She was also recently divorced and not convinced that Prince Charming was anywhere on the horizon. She added that she had recently met someone, but that it was too early to tell where that would lead.

I liked her. Actually, we really had a lot in common. We both had thriving careers, loved sports—and the outdoors. And both of us, it seems, had miserable track records when it came to relationships.

"I've been a doormat for too many men for far too long," Jennie said while sipping lemonade. "But I'm making a conscious effort now to change all that, and stand up for myself."

"Me too," I said. "I'm too much of a people-pleaser. I'm always trying to make someone else happy. From now on, I'm working on my OWN happiness."

I didn't bother to mention what I did or why I was there. And Jennie didn't ask. Actually, I prefer it that way. Sometimes it's a relief to be somewhere *without* a camera—to be recognized for who I am, and not just for what I do.

As usual, I had a deadline to meet. So I exchanged phone numbers with Jennie, then forged ahead alone.

By mid-afternoon I arrived in Des Moines and checked in immediately at the NBC satellite truck.

"Hey, Kristen," greeted Justin. "How's our biker chick?"

"Very funny," I replied. "Actually, I had a wonderful day. I got some good exercise, saw some beautiful scenery, and even made a friend. I almost forgot the terrible story we're covering."

"Speaking of which, John wants you to call him in New York right away. He says he has some new information."

"Thanks, Justin."

I reached for the phone and found John at his desk. "Hi, John. It's Kristen. What's up?"

"Kristen, we tracked down Tom Spurgeon's ex-wife. We know who she is and where she lives, but we can't seem to find her."

"Really?" My eyes widened.

"But we did get a picture of her from the Black Hawk County Courthouse," he continued. "I guess Tom Spurgeon roughed her up a couple of times a few years back. In fact, I'm faxing you the picture right now."

As the fax by the phone slowly spit out the picture, I gasped at what I saw. I not only gasped—I actually stopped breathing for a moment.

"Kristen, did you get the picture?"

I couldn't speak.

"Kristen, did you get the picture?"

Now my heart was REALLY racing, and I took a moment to catch my breath. "John?" I stammered.

"Yes?"

"John, I got the picture."

"Good."

"John—there's something else."

"What?"

"I don't know whether she's a suspect or the next victim, but Tom Spurgeon's ex-wife is our lead on the NBC Evening News tonight. Let's call it an exclusive."

AMY JOHNSON *is a veteran broadcast journalist and a veteran of RAGBRAI. She has worked as an anchor and reporter at KGAN-TV in Cedar Rapids for the past 12 years, and has ridden and reported on four of the last nine RAGBRAI's. Unlike Kristen Jensen, Amy is happy not to have the pressure of a network TV job—and is very happily married to radio personality and comedian Tim Boyle.*

8

Jim Wade's
Mid-Ride Meditation

By Carl H. Klaus

A new life. Or at least a new adventure. Or just a breath of fresh air. What else could have lured me into this crazy bike ride across Iowa? Oh yes, it's given me a well-needed break from the grind of mystery writing—grinding my way instead through the corn and beans, corn and beans, sweeping to the horizon. And it's definitely helped to get my mind off of Amy and her creepy foot doctor. And in a way, it's given me a bigger kick than a singles bar or a disco club, thanks to Jennie, who's filled my nights with so many dreams and my days with so many desires that I sometimes wish we could head off on our own journey and leave the bike ride forever behind us. Especially here amid the bridges of Madison County.

But otherwise, this marathon has mostly been like a kick in the pants, especially given my starring role in a murder mystery somebody else is writing, without giving me many clues as to who done it or how it might work out. And speaking of clues, I don't have the slightest idea of how things might work out with Jennie, given the on-again-off-again way it's been with her lately. One moonlit night, just an hour or so after we've met, she's sliding her arm through mine, telling me about the sadistic brutality of her former husband, telling me how eager she is to read some of my work, telling me in words as shy and roundabout as mine that we seem to have more things in common than our failed marriages. Then the lightning bugs seemed to be flickering in unison with my desires.

But the next day, after each of us has been interviewed by the highway patrol, she suddenly turns silent and more silent with every passing mile, until she's riding ahead of me, her pony tail waving in the distance, while I'm reduced to admiring her from afar, up and down the hilly roads of southwest Iowa. Then just as suddenly she's all smiles when we stop for lemonade and she meets up with her old college buddy and state trooper, Lars Loving, whose name's as implausible as his claim that he's just along for the ride. But when Lars is gone, we're hand in hand again, until she's off to her tentmate and I'm left to sleep in my uptight bedroll, alone under the stars.

And now on our way from Creston to Des Moines, she's riding right next to me, expressionless except for a slight smile at the edge of her lips. Maybe it's just because she's as shy and uncertain as I am after all these years with someone else—the wrongone else. But then again, like every woman I've ever known, she's a mystery beyond my comprehension, and I'm beginning to think she might be more in league with the highway patrol than she is with me. A double-agent for a sting operation they're planning to spring on me.

And it wasn't much different with that gung-ho blonde from the *Today Show*. Kristen Jensen—small-town girl now from the big city and the big-time TV program. All ears, all smiles, her eyelashes aflutter when she asked me to tell my side of the story. Her eyes bright, her head nodding eagerly as I answered her questions about the murder of Eyepatch. But completely deaf when I wanted to see her that evening. Then she suddenly turned cold and recriminating, her blue eyes glaring as if I'd asked her to shack up with me, when all I did was to ask her about getting together for a beer, so I could tell her about some of the things I didn't want to say on camera. Things like the sadistic glee of the Marvelaires and the cryptic cell phone conversation of Eyepatch a few hours before his demise and the knife scars Jennie showed me when she was talking about her former husband. I wanted to tell Kristen that there was more to the story than I had let on, more than even I, the so-called mystery writer, could figure out at present. Knives everywhere and no telling where the next ones might land. How strange in the midst of this bucolic landscape, cattle reclining under the shade of oak trees! But her cold stare told me in no uncertain terms that I'd broken a cardinal rule of her journalistic game—never to presume upon the familiarity of a network reporter, especially of the opposite sex, especially if you happen to be a murder suspect.

Given the way things have gone with Jennie and Kristen and the highway patrol, I'm beginning to feel like a sucker or a sadsack or just a misguided forty-eight-year-old male who doesn't know the first thing about the ins and outs of the modern-day mating game or the media game or any other escapade, including this murderous bike ride across Iowa. How else to account for the fact that I've been one of the prime suspects ever since the night of the murder, just because I happen to have been the one who discovered Eyepatch burning in his tent? A good Samaritan turned into a murder suspect, thank-you! And no matter what I say or do I can't seem to shake the role I've been cast in. As if I'd been set up by someone to take the fall for murdering the bastard, when all I wanted to do was get away from him the minute I first met him.

And who's to say I didn't kill Eyepatch? I don't, after all, have anyone who can vouch for my whereabouts at the time of the murder. No witness or companion sharing a tent with me like Jennie and her girl friend. Nothing but the dog, the mysterious mongrel—part German Shepherd, part something else—that came running out of Eyepatch's tent just when I arrived and dashed off into the woods by the park, like a horror-stricken beast. No wonder it cowered when it first caught sight of me. Only the dog might know what happened, and I could hardly expect a dog to serve as my witness, even if it could be found.

So, by a natural process of elimination, I, it seems, am the prime suspect. Maybe that's why Jennie sometimes puts such a distance between herself and me—maybe she thinks I did it, especially after talking with the state patrol. And the highway patrol certainly doesn't have a better suspect than me, not at least from their point of view, whereas I'm beginning to feel like I might be a prime target for the next murder. Especially if I'm not willing to take the rap for killing Eyepatch.

Talk about being victimized! It's gotten so bad that I'm now beginning to think that I might have done it myself, that my mind might have temporarily snapped, and that's why I can't figure this thing out, because I'm hiding the truth from myself. And if that's the case, then maybe I should just turn myself in and tell the detectives to give me the truth serum if they want to find out what really happened. Who knows what might come tumbling out of my mouth with a shot of sodium pentathol? But then again who knows what might come tumbling out of anyone's mouth with a shot of that stuff?

Come to think of it, I wonder what would come tumbling out of Eyepatch's cell phone if someone had found it and could make it replay the other side of the conversation. Who was it that called him, and why was he so impatient to hear from this person in the midst of the bike ride? If only that cell phone could be found and made to talk, then I'd be free to head off with Jennie to a new life for both of us. If only the dog could be found and made to talk. But it's a long way from here to Christmas Eve, when the animals speak at midnight.

Until then, I'm left to figure this thing out for myself, and who better to figure it out than a mystery writer like me? So, to begin at the beginning, a murder requires not only a murderer, but a motive. In other words, why would someone want to kill Eyepatch, aside from the fact that he was a creep, a complainer, and a sinister human being? Maybe because he was too sinister for the vanity of others, like the Marvelaires, especially Cap who might well have performed a bizarre ritual murder, outknifing Eyepatch, and then putting on a deadly knife display for all to see, as if defying the detectives to arrest him then and there at the campgrounds in Creston. Could Cap be the serial killer—masked and hiding on RAGBRAI?

But it could also be that Eyepatch was too sinister for the comfort of others, especially if there were others he might have been out to mutilate with his pearl-handled knives, say like some long-standing enemy or friend or cohort or lover. But who could possibly have been so involved with Eyepatch, except for another sadist like him? Perhaps a masochist—in love with the cruelty of his knives.

Such dark thoughts, such dark thoughts, here on this bright afternoon—the daylilies blooming along the roadside and Jennie riding by my side. I can hardly bear to continue for fear my mind might really snap before our journey's end.

CARL H. KLAUS, *founder and former director of the University of Iowa's Nonfiction Writing Program, is a diarist, essayist, and longtime Iowa City vegetable gardener. Dr. Klaus has taken stock of his garden, the weather, his life, and university life in* My Vegetable Love: A Journal of a Growing Season, Taking Retirement: A Beginner's Diary, *and* Weathering Winter: A Gardener's Daybook.

9
Hot Water
By Thomas A. Fogarty

Lars Loving's knees burned as he churned up the steep gravel road leading north out of Winterset. For once, though, the wide, knobby tires on the bicycle he bought in Shenandoah were working to his advantage. They slowed him on pavement, but the knobbies were just made for gravel which wreaks havoc on those skinny road-bike tires. After an excruciating mile-long climb, Loving reached the top of the hill and a long, reasonably flat stretch of pavement.

Click. Click. Click. Click. Click.

God, how Lars loved the sound: the dense pack of bicyclists surrounding him, each upshifting almost in unison as they crested the hill. If people don't ride, Loving thought, they don't understand what a mechanical marvel the modern bicycle is.

Maybe there's a book in it, he thought. *Zen and the Art of Bicycle Maintenance?*

Tall, blond and buff, Loving was an awkward sight on the

undersized mountain bike. Finding any bike in Shenandoah had turned out to be an accomplishment. The best he could do in the picked-over selection of the bicycle-crazed town was the $139 Huffy he found at Wal-Mart.

Huffies are the ultimate kids' knock-around bike. After two days on the road, the bicycle was performing surprisingly well. The worst part—other than not being able to lift the seat quite high enough for comfort—was putting up with the taunts.

"Hey, Huffy, outta my way," yelled some wise-acre kid zipping past on a sleek Bianchi.

"Get a life," Loving muttered.

Loving had been feeling increasingly discouraged about the investigation. Lt. Dallas seemed to think it was a master stroke to put him on the ride undercover. In fact, Loving was getting nowhere. It wasn't that nobody was talking. The problem was that everyone was talking. The murder was the buzz everywhere he turned. Ten thousand riders with nothing to do but yammer and gossip all day. Everyone had some kind of crazy theory to offer. Facts were elusive.

Loving once found wise words in Buddist philosophy that had served him well in police work : "Those who say, don't know. Those who know, don't say."

Just then, two women on a tandem passed Loving, speaking what he recognized as Japanese. He made out just two words of their conversation: "Eyepatch" and "daggers."

Needles and haystacks.

At about 3 o'clock, Loving rolled into Cumming. The tiny burg was throbbing. It was the last stop before the overnight in Des Moines, and the owners of the Tip-Top Tap—the Harkin boys—made sure the beer kept flowing in an outdoor beverage garden.

The skies were fair, the weather mild, and the overnight stop was just 12 short miles beyond Cumming. The bicyclists had the day pretty well licked, and it was time to kick back.

Outside the tavern, a guy was making a killing by selling "I ♥ Cumming" T-shirts. Loving watched a middle-aged guy with white spiky hair—a Californian, no doubt—peel off $120 for 10 T-shirts.

"I got people back home who aren't going to believe this shirt," the spiky guy said.

In 22 years as an Iowan, the double entendre of the town's name had never occurred to Loving.

On the roped-off main drag, a dee-jay was blasting a smutty r&b tune—"Strokin'." Loving had heard this Clarence Carter song, which is set to an unshakably catchy tune, at beer gardens in Corning, Prescott, Creston, and Lorimor. A RAG-BRAI anthem, Loving concluded.

At the Cumming fest, a hundred or so bicyclists engaged in an intricately choreographed line dance, singing and swaying to "Strokin'."

"Strokin' to the east, strokin' to the west, strokin' to the one that I love best." The crowd went wild.

Some of the old-timers in the line dance probably spend the other 51 weeks a year fretting about the influence of rap lyrics on their teenaged kids, Lars figured. What the hell. This is RAGBRAI.

The bone-tired state trooper knew he should be working the crowd, squeezing out whatever small pieces of info might help find Eyepatch's killer. Instead, he snagged a long-neck and found a shaded, relatively quiet patch of grass along the side of the tavern. Back against the brick wall, Loving squatted on his heels. Elbows on his knees, he pinched the top of his beer bottle between thumb and forefinger, swinging it gently.

Apparently others felt the need to escape the din of Main Street. A man—an older fellow—and four women, plopped onto the grass nearby. The man, whose shock of white hair stood in contrast to his deeply red sunburned face, wore plaid shorts and a Chicago Cubs T-shirt. He looked like he might be more at home vacationing in Branson, Missouri, than on RAGBRAI.

The women were much younger than the man, but each had been on the planet long enough to develop some character to her face. Each had a body that was hard and lean from biking. They looked great in spandex, Loving thought.

Loving didn't need to be a trained investigator to figure out this group. The women were wearing matching tanktops. On the back was a picture of the white-haired guy and the name "Team Larry."

The white-haired fellow—presumably the namesake and van driver for "Team Larry"—was clearly a man who relished the company of younger women. From his blather—

clearly audible—Loving deduced that Larry was a retired newspaperman. The women—Lynn, Birdie, Holli, and Deb—revealed themselves in the conversation also to be newsies of some sort.

"There's something weird about this Eyepatch deal," said Larry. "In the 1970s, I was working at the *Chicago Sun-Times*. A federal grand jury was investigating a bunch of guards at the prison in Joliet, who were getting rich by supplying dope and whores to the inmates. I was kickin' ass on the story.

"I had a source who worked as a guard at the prison. He knew I was from Muscatine, and that was his hometown, too. A screwy reason for trusting a reporter, but that's why he'd talk to me. One day, the calls stopped coming, and I never heard from the guy again. I sidled up to a friend of mine in the D.A.'s office, just to make sure my guy was still okay.

"He told me my guy was fine, that 'Uncle' had taken care of him. I assume that meant the feds took him into the witness protection program, but I don't know that for sure.

"Now here's the weird part: My guy was named Tim Sturgeon. The news said Eyepatch was named Thomas Michael Spurgeon, and that he had worked at the pen in Joliet. Strange, huh?"

Strange indeed, thought Loving. No need to engage Team Larry in conversation now, though. Loving noticed they were wearing wristbands. That meant the team was registered with the RAGBRAI office if he should need to get more info from them later.

If Spurgeon—or Sturgeon—were in the witness protection program, Loving knew the feds would never volunteer the information to the State Patrol. Loving decided he'd drop a dime on his old friend Mike Giardello when he got to Des Moines. Giardello was a buddy from Loving's days at bomb school at Quantico. "Gee," as fellow cops called him, was working now as the F.B.I. liaison to the Baltimore police department. If there's anything to this Sturgeon-Spurgeon thing, Loving thought, Gee could sort things out.

Frazzled from the road, the women didn't seem to be paying much attention to old Larry's rambling narrative.

"Where we eating tonight?" Holli asked.

Jennie and Jim had made good time on the 71-mile trip from Creston to Des Moines. By the third day of the ride, they appeared to have become inseparable. They decided to bypass the zaniness in Cumming. Bodies can take only so much.

By mid-afternoon, they'd reached the grounds of the Iowa Capitol, the overnight stop for RAGBRAI. They rolled in early enough to get a prime camping spot among the monuments on the south side of the Capitol. Theirs was a flat swath of zoysia next to the bust of Christopher Columbus, which, according to the inscription, was erected by the Italian Americans of Iowa in 1938.

Perfect. Sycamores overhead. A short distance to tote the camping gear to and from the big Register semi that carries mountains of luggage from one overnight town to the next. The port-a-potties—probably 80 of them—were lined up along Walnut Street. They were far enough away from Jim and Jennie so as not to stink, and close enough so that relieving themselves wouldn't become a chore.

Their view of the graceful old Capitol building was not from its most flattering side. From the south, too many trees screened out too many of its architectural features. But the big center dome and two of the building's four cupolas, all regilded to a shiny splendor in 1999, were fully visible. Jim took comfort in just being near the grand old building which he had loved since he first visited it on a school field trip in seventh grade.

"I saw a sign that said they've opened Lucas Elementary for showers," said Jim. "It's just east of here a few blocks."

"Probably cold, even this early in the day," said Jennie.

"Let's get the tent up and head over there to try our luck," he responded. The evening was filled with promise. Last night in Creston, Jennie told her female traveling companion that she'd be staying in Jim's tent in Des Moines.

Said Jennie: "I saw a T-shirt today out on the road that said, 'Just because I slept with you last night doesn't mean I have to ride with you today.' Guess we've kinda flipped that around."

Buried somewhere in Jennie's gear, a cellular telephone began to ring. She rummaged and fumbled.

"Damn, how does this thing work? . . . Hello . . . Hello."

"Jennie, this is Kristen Jensen . . . Remember? From the square in Winterset."

"Hi."

"I saw your cell phone and took town your number. I didn't tell you this earlier, but I'm a reporter for NBC News. I need to talk to you. Where are you?"

"The battery in my phone is getting . . ." Jennie punched the power button.

"Who was that?" Jim asked quietly.

"Wrong number. Let's get over to Lucas while there's still hot water."

THOMAS A. FOGARTY *has covered government, politics, and business for the* Des Moines Register *since 1985. Earlier, he was a reporter at the* Lincoln Journal *and the* Kansas City Star. *He's ridden seven RAGBRAIs. In August 1999, following RAGBRAI and the completion of this chapter, he moved to Washington D.C. to begin a new job as a business writer for* USA Today.

IO

Sex and Religion

By Jan McLinn

It wasn't uncommon for the riders of RAGBRAI to choose to remain rather anonymous regarding their lives the remaining fifty-one weeks of the year. After all, RAGBRAI offered the opportunity to find that much needed relief from the demands they faced daily in their careers, as well as from their parenting challenges and all the other day-to-day grinds that made the week on RAGBRAI one as eagerly anticipated as a tropic island getaway when Iowa temperatures plummet to twenty below each winter. RAGBRAI promises each participant the chance to be someone else, really any person one chooses to be for just that week in time.

With new teams developing each and every RAGBRAI, many charter participants were always eager to check out the new groups. RAGBRAI mainstays wanted to know as much as possible about the makeup of each team. Who these people were, what they did, where they were from, and what brought them together as a group to spend this week on a bike trek across the state of Iowa? And some inquiring minds with more selfish motives would also wonder: are they married, are they professionals, and would they be interested in a relationship? And if interested, would that be a relationship for just the week of RAGBRAI, or perhaps something more long term?

Thus the interest targeted on one particular group of six male bikers—a group appearing unattached and possibly even ready to meet Ms. Right. The men dominated the thoughts of Angi Gales, best friend and tent-mate of Jennie Wyman—up until Jennie's moving out this morning to share something more promising with her new companion, Jim Wade. Angie decided that if Jennie, with her many odd moods and unusual quirks (especially of late) could find love and romance on RAGBRAI, then even she, Angi Gales, should be able to find a man (or even men) to spend the remaining four days with, and maybe even longer.

The men in question, and Angi felt any of the group would prove worthy, had just joined the bike trek in Des Moines, and, according to rumors she heard through other riders, would only participate until Saturday morning due to other obligations.

Angi was generally very good at what she did. And when truly driven, she could accomplish the impossible. Therefore, Angi was not the least bit concerned about the time constraints, or about the mysteries surrounding this group of appealing but enigmatic men.

The new team that seemed to attract not only the attention of Angi, but also the curiosity of everyone, called itself "Team Fatherhood." Wearing black T-shirts emblazoned with the team's name both on the front and back, this new group of mid-RAGBRAI riders consisted of six men, all from the state of Iowa, and the majority from the northern Iowa area. All were athletically inclined and extremely driven, and they appeared to have a bond with one another that indicated a brotherhood from days gone by.

Some riders speculated the six were brothers, but one quick glance quickly showed there was no chance these men could be related. Another suggestion was that they were fraternity brothers, continuing on with their college escapades of years gone by. But from the obvious age variances of the six it was apparent the men were not all classmates at the same time. Others speculated that since the team was called "Team Fatherhood" then perhaps they were all divorced fathers. Perhaps they met in a support group, and perhaps that support group then decided to form a team and participate in RAGBRAI. That made as much sense as any of the other ideas. Of course, the most obvious approach would simply be to ask them, but then speculating about the other teams was half the fun.

What brought them together didn't seem to concern Angi. She really didn't care. All she knew is that she was on a mission, and that mission was to find a man, for three days or three decades! At this point, she laughingly thought, even three hours would probably do it. (However, the pathetic three minutes she frequently experienced from her last lover were not nearly adequate according to Angi's standards.)

Ever since walking in on Jennie and Jim last night in what Angi would longingly term "the heat of passion," Angi had decided that she, too, would pursue hot, steamy memories of RAGBRAI—and she wasn't referring to the humid days spent pedaling. She wanted to add romance to her RAGBRAI memoirs.

Although Angi tried unsuccessfully to forget the scene she had interrupted when she excitedly bounded into the tent she and Jennie shared to announce news of an impromptu RAGBRAI party at the river nearby, she knew what she witnessed between Jennie and Jim, even in that one quick embarrassed glimpse, only fueled the embers of her own burning needs (not to mention the flames of her self-doubt and self-esteem).

Angi didn't consider herself a loose woman, but more a "Woman of the New Millennium." Although she did not necessarily believe in one night stands, she did feel that if two people ended up together and had a lot in common, and if they had a great time together, and, well, that's what it led to, the bedroom, well then, that was okay. Of course, being single in a group of friends that were either married or divorced, and some with children, she had learned early on that many of her peers did not share her feelings on the issue of "casual encounters" (much less tacky than the term "casual sex," she thought smugly).

With her mind made up, Angi actually paced herself during the ride Wednesday, always attempting to ride somewhat behind this new group of "qualifying" men, always ready with a smile or an interesting expression should they look back her way. "At least a few of them must be available," she thought to herself as she concentrated on her plans for the evening. No matter what brought Team Fatherhood together, Angi was confident she could infiltrate the group and find a partner for fun—and anything else that might unfold.

RAGBRAI officials, on the other hand, were completely aware of what the members of Team Fatherhood had in common. Although choosing to keep their vocations anonymous during their three days of biking vacation, the six priests felt it was vital officials knew they were men of the cloth—just in case their services were needed. With a vocation in which you are basically "punched in" 365 days a year, 24 hours a day, you knew it was your responsibility to alert those in charge of your clergy status . . . just in case!

And with the shocking events that transpired the first few days of the ride, the six "brothers" felt perhaps that what they once envisioned as a relaxing form of recreation for six good friends could indeed require their special services as they joined the trek from Des Moines to Grinnell and then on to Cedar Rapids.

Angi's opportunity to move in on her targets arrived during the evening as the group arrived in Grinnell. The six men making up Team Fatherhood were setting up their campsite as Angi, with her best smile and most revealing crop-top and spandex shorts, sauntered up to offer what she considered her most charming small talk.

"Hi, I'm Angi Gales," she said. "I guess we'll be campmates," she added, demurely offering her recently manicured hand, speaking in the most ladylike tone she could muster after spending the entire day riding 70 miles in rain and mist, and then hurriedly using a community shower to primp and prepare herself for this new role as seductress.

One man stepped forward and made the introductions, "My name is Michael O'Connor, but call me Mike. This is Carl Flannery, Jim O'Malley, David McCarthy, Dennis O'Doul and Ken McGuire."

Small talk followed. Remaining as charming and coy as she could, Angi learned that the six men were all from North Iowa, and would only be riding on RAGBRAI through Saturday morning, as their schedules all posed conflicts for the remainder of the upcoming weekend. They all worked together, she learned, and their headquarters was located in Dubuque.

Angi was encouraged by this announcement as she envisioned these men must be in highly important positions, possibly doctors, to have to meet such tight schedules when trying to get away for just one tiny week of the year. She also noticed the attention paid to them by RAGBRAI officials. Always stopping to make certain the group was having fun—did they need anything?—just let an official know if they did! There was respect for these guys, and it certainly did not go unnoticed by Angi.

Her active imagination ran away with her as she thought about the city of Dubuque—how it would be a wonderful city to settle down in and raise a family. Angi quickly ruled out her short term prospects and immediately shifted into her long-term relationship mode. Time to talk about things that single, divorced men would like to hear a woman talking about.

Mike and Carl announced they would be making a beer run, and Angi quickly offered to assist them in carrying back enough beer for the evening. Exchanging somewhat surprised glances and grinning as though they found something amusing in her offer, the men set off with Angi for the nearest Casey's.

Returning thirty minutes later, the amused faces of the two priests, Father Mike and Father Carl, paled in comparison to the mortified expression on the face of Angi Gales. In the brief walk to retrieve what amounted to two six packs of "the least expensive beer on sale" as ordered by Father Carl, Angi had used every line she knew and some she just made up along the way, and following a number of no fail come-ons which she knew would let them know she was ready (okay, more than ready), willing and able, she learned that "Team Fatherhood" represented neither a den of divorced daddies nor a clique of fraternity brothers, but rather a contingent of six Catholic priests needing a few days of R & R before returning to their individual parishes to serve in their chosen vocations.

Returning to the group, Angi hastily downed her beer, bid farewell to the amused but understanding men, and made a hasty retreat to relive her moment of humiliation in private and lick her wounds. As she stumbled across the lawn in search of someone to talk to, she caught sight of Jennie Wyman strolling alone, without her new constant companion, Jim Wade. Although Jennie seemed preoccupied and somewhat troubled, Angi was compelled to unload on her best friend what had just transpired with the six priests.

"Jen," Angi called, "Wait up!"

The two shared bits and pieces of the past few days, including Angi's commentary on Jennie's newfound romance with Jim. When Angi tried to make light of stumbling upon the two in the tent, Jennie added very little to the conversation, and at many times seemed distraught and even near tears. Angi then revealed her latest faux pas involving "Team Fatherhood" thinking that sharing the irony of her blunder might cheer her friend up, even if it would be at Angi's own expense.

"Can you believe it, Jen?" she asked laughingly, finally finding a bit of humor in the fact that she had just provided six men of the cloth with everything they probably already had heard in the confessional. "I mean, here there were six nice-looking guys—no wedding rings—what else was I supposed to think? I just can't believe I actually hit on a group of priests," she added.

Although Jennie seemed to be listening to Angi's play-by-play, her concentration seemed to be on other things. Angi continued with her story, finding it more humorous by the minute, yet noticing that Jennie's attention was definitely not on the conversation at hand.

Finally Angi, feeling somewhat disconcerted by Jennie's lack of interest, said, "Jennie, we used to be able to share stories and secrets, and we were such good friends. But something has changed with you. You're so distant, and so up and down, I guess I just want to know if it's something I've done? Please tell me what it was and I will apologize or try and make it right."

Angi and Jennie's friendship went back as far as the days of Jennie's abusive relationship with her ex-husband. Angi wondered, has Jennie again jumped into a relationship with this Jim without knowing much about him, and is this another volatile, abusive association in which Jennie has again assumed the role of victim? Perhaps Jennie had again put herself into a rocky affair with a man with a dark side, and this time perhaps she needed out before things got way out of hand.

Jennie took Angi's hands in her own and said, "No, Angi, it's absolutely nothing you have done. I know I can always count on you. It's something that I just need to deal with on my own—without your help, or any other help. I just need to figure out some things and need some time, okay? I am just so sorry to be this way, but I need to get through this by myself."

The two women hugged, and then, trying her best to sound as sincere as she could, Jennie said, "So Angi, you hit on six priests, huh? How'd you do?"

The two friends spent a few more minutes laughing about Angi's latest escapade, and then each returned to her individual stroll.

Father Michael O'Connor tidied up the Team Fatherhood's campsite prior to an evening walk. Although the remaining five priests had retired early following the first day of their RAGBRAI journey, Father Mike felt restless and not ready for sleep. Strolling along the streets of Grinnell he contemplated the events which had transpired earlier that evening. A very attractive woman had made a pass at, well, all of them. He shook his head with a smile. How do you explain to people that sometimes you just need to be away from the vocation—that you just need to be a regular guy participating in RAGBRAI? And yet, by assuming this anonymity, the group also had opened itself to many new, unfamiliar situations, including those that affect other single men when thrown together with single women. The irony, of course, was that their lives were dedicated to God and the Church. This was their love; however this brief stint on RAGBRAI was their opportunity to, yes, talk as priests to one another, but also to act like regular guys challenging each other to the RAGBRAI experience. And in the process, maybe meet some people, make some friends, and perhaps discover distinct parallels in the sense of community so evident among the RAGBRAI participants and the sense of community within their parishes.

Pausing to reflect on his life and chosen vocation, Father Mike felt a sense of contentment and peace. He was doing what he was called to do, as were his friends back at the campsite. As far as their participation on RAGBRAI, Mike smiled and thought, God only knows what the next two days will bring.

Returning to the campsite, Father Mike was just preparing to turn in when a man's voice startled him.

"Father? Can I talk to you Father?"

Turning to face the man, Father Mike was startled to see a look of anguish on the face of the man before him.

"Father, I am Catholic, and I overheard you and your friends talking and I know you are priests."

Father Mike nodded and the man proceeded.

"The thing is, Father, although I am Catholic, I'm not a very good one. I've been divorced, and I've sinned—more times than we have time to talk about. But something really big has happened, and I guess I need some help, some guidance. Please, could I talk to you?"

Father Mike nodded, and the two men began walking along the same path from which Father Mike had just returned.

"I guess this is kinda like a confession. I really don't know what to do. I guess I'm just lost. But what I tell you is just between us, okay?"

Father Mike nodded and added whatever encouragement

he could. His years in the priesthood had trained him for almost any situation, and he had also learned that patience and time were often needed in these circumstances. Therefore, he was totally unprepared for the next words which tumbled from the man's mouth.

JAN MCLINN *is a freelance writer for the* Mason City Globe-Gazette. *She has been an Advertising Director for Metalcraft, Inc., a northern Iowa manufacturing company. Her current vocation is wife, mother, and volunteer. She serves on the Parish Council with both a Fr. Carl and a Fr. Mike; volunteers at her children's school, Newman Catholic; and assists with fund-raising and volunteers for the Stebens Children's Theatre. Jan is on the board of the North Iowa Chapter of the Alliance for the Mentally Ill and has also been involved with the American Cancer Society, United Way of Cerro Gordo County, North Iowa Girl Scout Council, and a number of other associations. She lives in Mason City with her husband, Dave, and their two children, Pat, 13, and Jenny, almost 10.*

II

Leave Things Better Than You Found Them

By Matthew V. Clemens

Darkness clenched Ahrens Park in its black fist, and 10,000 bikers were settled into their beds, cots, and sleeping bags for the night. But not before Grinnell had lavished them with attention. The throng had ridden in on U.S. Highway 6, made its way along Sixth Avenue to Penrose, then turned left to Ahrens, the largest of the nine parks in town. There they'd been met by members of the Fraternal Order of Eagles Aerie #2545 who sold them box chicken dinners, while Pagliai's Pizza had turned out with what seemed like hundreds of discount pies.

The Rec Center had been opened for those who wanted to shower, and the Family Center had granted the riders, at least those not too exhausted from the day's ride, a chance to take a dip in its pool. After that, some of the riders had watched the girls' softball games or played like children on the vast wood and plastic jungle gym that dominated the southwest side of the park.

Now though, Lt. Scott Dallas noted as he stood in front of the bronze statue at the park's west entrance, the riders were down for the night. The statue depicted a happy, smiling family: father, mother, and young son. A line of old fashioned glass-domed street lights provided enough light for Dallas to read the words carved in the statue's base. "Leave Things Better Than You Found Them," surrounded a globe etched into the bronze.

Fat chance, Dallas thought as he marched north toward the Rec Center. The entire investigation was fubar (fouled up beyond all reason), and had been since the beginning. He considered the last five days and decided he should have gone to the governor immediately and had this whole bike ride canceled, postponed at the very least. His first mistake, and there had been plenty since, he told himself, had been not to close the park that very first morning.

Even then, with 16,000 suspects, he'd had little chance of nailing Tom Spurgeon's killer. And that was if the culprit had even been on the ride to begin with. The killer could just as easily have strolled into the park in the middle of the night, slain Spurgeon, and walked right back out without anyone even noticing. After all, you didn't end up in the witness protection program if you hadn't already pissed off somebody.

Dallas had hoped the walk around the park would help ease his tension, but it had only increased his frustration.

With each step among the sleeping bikers another bungle attacked his brain. He hadn't had the personnel to surround the entire horde. Even if the killer had stayed with the group, there was nothing to prevent him from just riding off into the sunset anywhere along the route. No one would have been the wiser.

The good news was Zenith had finally caught up with them. The bad news was the canvassing of Shenandoah had added zip to the investigation, and Zenith still seemed peeved over not receiving the serial killer information from his Lieutenant. But Dallas hadn't figured Spurgeon's death to be the work of the Eye Doctor. He hated the nicknames the FBI used for these monsters, but they all seemed to have one, and this animal that planted knives in the eye sockets of his victims had been dubbed the Eye Doctor by some less than sensitive Fed. Dallas had already heard enough Pearle Vision jokes to last him a lifetime.

Though Spurgeon had the requisite pearl-handled knives protruding from his eyes, he also had his tongue—something removed from the Eye Doctor's victims. That one fact, closely guarded by the F.B.I. and known only to a handful of other officers, told Dallas that Spurgeon's murderer was simply a copycat and that was why he hadn't passed the information on to Zenith. Hathaway had confirmed Dallas' suspicion with his report that Spurgeon had been killed by a stab wound to the heart and not by the knives to the eyes.

Dallas also questioned his decision about Lars Loving. Putting the young trooper undercover had seemed like a good plan at the time, but now Dallas just shook his head. It wasn't like the kid was dogging it. Loving had talked to many of the riders along the route—but to no avail.

Trudging through the darkness, weaving between tents and sleeping bags, Dallas came to the realization that he'd need a miracle to solve this case. With only three days to go, he didn't seem to know any more about Spurgeon's killer than he did on that first day.

To his left Dallas heard a low grunt, then what sounded like a woman moan. He froze. No one around him stirred. He couldn't tell exactly where the sound had come from. How far had it carried in the quiet night air? Three paces to his left, Dallas touched the trunk of a pine tree. His right hand felt instinctively for the .38 on his right hip and he silently released the snap. Ears straining to pick up any wrong sound on the slight breeze, he heard nothing. He stood perhaps a hundred yards from the nearest street light and he could barely make out the outlines of the nearby tents.

Sweat trickling down his back now, popping out on his forehead, Dallas crept two more steps into the trees that marked the northern border of the park. Another grunt, another moan, and he stood not ten paces from the tent the noises came from. Dallas lifted the .38 from its holster. The pistol felt heavy in his hand, like justice, he thought as his left hand came up to support it. Another step, his heart thudding against the walls of his chest so loud he was sure the whole park heard it, and another step; then another grunt and a moan.

"Oh, baby," a woman's voice pealed. "Yes, yes, yes!"

In one smooth step, Dallas came up, pistol locked in shooting position. Then as he realized the nature of the sounds, he sagged against a tree, holstered his pistol with one hand while covering his mouth with the other. The hysterical laugh of a madman bubbled to the surface. He swallowed it, and tried to move away as quietly as he could.

"Baby, did you hear something outside?" Dallas heard the woman ask.

"Naw," her companion said, his voice loud in the sleeping park. "Now let me get some sleep."

Dallas held it together until he stepped inside the door of the Rec Center. His sides hurt he laughed so hard. It seemed a strange sound to him, like a foreign language he hadn't heard spoken in years. Not a man who laughed easily, Dallas knew the torrent of giggles to be a warning that he was close to losing it. RAGBRAI was supposed to be a cush assignment, a reward. It certainly didn't feel like that now.

His hysteria under control, he stepped back out into the night and looked to the south. Beyond the far end of the park he saw the lights of the DeKalb seed plant. Dallas took a deep breath in through his nose, held it a moment, then released it slowly through his mouth. After repeating the action two more times, he resumed his walk, this time turning east.

Silently, he checked off everything they'd done up till now. Considering there seemed to be no way to stop this wandering roadshow, Dallas felt confident they hadn't overlooked any obvious leads. Believing that he could make his own luck as well as have it fall into his lap, he knew he needed a break, but he had no idea how to create one.

The campers on this side of the Rec Center were even farther from the street lights at the front of the park. A bean field lay to the north, a corn field to the east, and the softball diamonds to the south. Only a hundred or so riders had chosen to wedge themselves into this area of the park.

Dallas moved slowly and quietly through the tents and sleeping bags, careful not to trip over stray tent lines. The smell of grass being smoked slipped into his nostrils and he allowed himself a self-conscious smile. He wished this was the biggest problem he faced. The smile vanished almost immediately as the weight of reality settled back on his shoulders.

Again Dallas heard moans to his left. This time, he felt more like a voyeur than a state trooper. As he neared the noises he was able to make out two outlines against the moonlight. One shape loomed over a prone body. He turned to move silently away when he heard the unmistakable snick of a switchblade being opened. Spinning, his right hand freeing the .38 from its holster even as he saw his first glimpse of the knife poised at the top of its arc, reflecting the moonlight.

"Freeze," he snapped, his voice as cold as the single word he uttered.

A masked face turned to him in the darkness, the white

teeth shining like those of a carnivore surprised as it was about to deliver the killing blow to its prey.

Dallas repeated his warning, more loudly this time. "Freeze!"

The face started to turn back to its grisly task, the knife beginning its downward arc as Dallas pumped two slugs into the back of the attacker. The blade flew from the masked man's hand as he slumped to one side. To Dallas the man fell in slow motion. The sudden muzzle flash in the pitch dark caused Dallas to see stars as he watched the attacker's body hitting the ground like the throwing of a switch that caused the park to erupt in a cacophonous barrage of noise and light.

Even as flashlights played around him like tiny search-lights at a Hollywood premiere, Dallas checked the pulse of the man he'd just shot, and found none. People screamed and yelled, their voices barely registering in the Lieutenant's head. Turning to the masked man's intended victim, Dallas looked into the pasty face of a wide-eyed middle-aged man.

"You all right?" Dallas asked.

The man nodded vaguely as if answering a voice much further away.

Dallas helped the man sit up. "Are you sure you're okay?"

The man nodded again, this time his eyes focusing on Dallas.

A squad car squealed across the parking lot in front of the Rec Center, rollers on, headlights carving the darkness, blinding Dallas for an instant. Hassell piled out, Zenith two steps behind, both of them with guns drawn.

Dallas held up his hands. "It's under control."

"What happened?" Hassell asked.

Pointing to the masked man, the headlights showing him to be wearing some sort of red, white and blue costume, Dallas said nothing.

Hassell said, "Jesus," and moved to the dead man's side.

Dallas turned back to the victim. "Can you tell me your name?"

"Father . . ." he gulped, started over. "Father Mike O'Connor. I'm from Dubuque."

"Do you know this man?"

"Is he . . .?" Father O'Connor asked while trying to peer around Dallas to see the body.

The Lieutenant just shook his head and stayed between the priest and the corpse.

Finally, Father O'Connor shook his head. "He just came up to me about ten minutes ago. He said he needed to confess."

"Confess what?" Dallas asked.

"That's sacred, Officer. You know that."

"Even after he tried to kill you?"

The priest offered no response.

A crowd was gathering around them and Dallas decided he needed somewhere quieter to question the priest. "How about you and I go into the Rec Center and get a cup of coffee?"

Father O'Connor nodded numbly.

Dallas wondered if the man was going into shock. He'd

seen it happen before in situations like this. Inside the building, Dallas poured them each a cup of coffee from the giant
urns filled for the riders and found them two chairs in an
empty office.

"You sure you don't want to tell me about this?"

"It was supposed to be a confession."

"Confessions don't usually end with a murder attempt,
do they?"

The priest set his styrofoam cup on the edge of the desk
and wiped both hands over his face. "No," he said, his voice
tiny even inside the small office, "they don't."

"But you don't want to . . ."

The words rushed out of O'Connor's mouth. "He said
he'd just killed someone."

"Did he say who?"

O'Connor sipped his coffee. Dallas watched the man's
hands shake as he set the cup back on the desk. Loving
strode into the office clad only in biker's shorts, his Glock
hanging loosely in his right hand against his thigh. Next to
him stood the mystery writer, Jim Wade. Dallas held up a
hand to keep the two men silent.

Finally, Father O'Connor went on. "All he would say was
that he killed a woman. Then he explained in great detail
how he did it. He . . . he . . . s . . . said . . . ." The father's
words trailed off into a moan he muffled by covering his
face with his hands.

Dallas rose, put a hand on the priest's shoulder. "Thank
you, Father. That's all for now."

The Lieutenant led Loving and Wade into the Rec Center's basketball court. "What have you got?"

"I think the woman that man just mentioned," Loving said, his voice low.

"Yeah?"

"The NBC camera crew went to get their reporter, Kristen Jensen."

Dallas nodded that he knew who Loving meant.

"They found her in her tent, knives protruding from both eyes."

"Damnation," Dallas said, his words more of foreboding of the oncoming media blitz than surprise over the reporter's death. Looking toward Wade, Dallas asked, "What's he doing here?"

"I remembered something about Spurgeon," Wade said.

Dallas blew out a long breath. "Yeah?"

"He had a cell phone. He used it that night—at dinner. The night he died."

"That could be something," Dallas allowed. "Did you see it that night when you tried to pull him from the tent?"

The writer shook his head.

"It wasn't in his effects. Where the hell did it go?"

The three men looked at each other for a long moment. Dallas nearly jumped when his cell phone chirped in his pocket. He pulled it out and flipped it open. "What?"

"It's Zenith," came the voice on the other end.

"Yeah?"

"I'm over by the softball field. "We've got a dead body. A

woman same as Spurgeon, knives through the eyes."

"Kristen Jensen?"

"Nope," Zenith said. "I've seen her on TV. This is another woman. One difference from Spurgeon though. She's got her tongue cut out."

"Damn it," Dallas whispered. Two things crystallized for him in that instant. One was that Captain America was the Eye Doctor and he'd just killed him. The second thing, the one that chilled Dallas to his soul, was that another killer remained among the thousands of riders in the park. Someone who would almost certainly try to kill again.

Hassell came in from outside. "Local cops are here."

Dallas nodded. "Let them secure the scene and take care of the bodies."

Hassell nodded, then with his brow furrowed, he asked, "Bodies?"

"Mr. Wade, will you fill him in please?"

Wade nodded.

"Lars."

"Yes, sir?"

"I want these riders up and out of here as soon as possible."

"Boss, it's 4:30 in the morning."

"I know," Dallas said, "but sitting here they're targets; on the move they're safe."

"Got it," Loving said and left the room.

Alone now, Dallas tried to straighten it all out in his mind. Captain America, the Eye Doctor, killed the woman down by the softball field, confessed to O'Connor, then Dallas had shot the serial killer as he tried to murder the priest. Someone else, the copycat, had killed Kristen Jensen and Tom Spurgeon, but Dallas had no motive, thousands of suspects, and only one clue. He needed to track down the phone records for Spurgeon's cellular phone. Then he needed to find the phone. Whoever had that phone had already murdered twice. Looking at the globe on the wall, Dallas once again read the words surrounding it: "Leave Things Better Than You Found Them."

He wished he could.

MATTHEW V. CLEMENS *is co-author of the true crime book* Dead Water: The Klindt Affair, *and is also president of Robin Vincent Publishing LLC. His short story "Family Values" appeared in the Signet anthology* Private Eyes *edited by Mickey Spillane and Max Allan Collins. He lives in Davenport with his wife, Pam, and three cats: Snuka, Siskel and Ebert.*

12

The Rider from the West

By John Johnson

One of the several thousand RABGRAI stories in the year 2000 belonged to a late-thirtyish man from Denver, Colorado. He was in good physical shape and rode a top-of-the-line mountain bike on this, his third ride across Iowa. He liked the blend of physical exercise, good food, casual companionship, and time away from the routine of hustling contracts and customer troubleshooting for his internet service accounts. But he got more than he bargained for this July. He had witnessed a murder.

He had been outside the tent in Shenandoah on the first night of the ride when Tom Spurgeon was killed. And he saw who did it. Ironically, the rider from Denver had had "conversations" with Tom Spurgeon on the last day of Spurgeon's life—although he didn't know his name at the time and had not volunteered his own. Spurgeon had seen him using his laptop computer at a beer break and yelled: "Hey, you damn yuppie, those don't belong on RAGBRAI."

Later he caught Spurgeon talking on his cell phone and taunted him, "Now who's the yuppie?"

Spurgeon just laughed and gave him the finger. He didn't have the heart to tell Spurgeon that he carried a cell phone too. In any case, that was the sum total of his interaction with the murder victim. A normal person would have unloaded his information on the Spurgeon killing to Lt. Scott Dallas or to one of the earnest young Iowa troopers. Or he might have fled the scene and never returned to the land of corn and soybeans. But this man wasn't normal. He was bright, well-educated, ran a successful business, and could on occasion be quite charming. But, as a shrink had once told him, he was "maladaptive." He just didn't do what was right or expected. And he couldn't be trusted to tell the truth.

So, after witnessing the killing, he didn't talk or run. He just continued to ride along quietly with the thousands of others, eavesdropping on the gossip about Spurgeon's death.

The real name of our rider from the West isn't important. In fact, when he indulged in his solitary but expensive holidays, he usually picked a pseudonym appropriate to the adventures. For example, when he took a tour of the Greek Islands he assumed the name of "Nicholas Urfe," the main character in John Fowles's erotic classic, *The Magus*. When he spent a fortnight playing the great golf courses of Scotland he called himself "Eugenio Saraceni," the real name of golfing legend Gene Sarazen. And when he hiked the foothills of Denali he was "Bill Seward," after the American Secretary of State responsible for purchasing Alaska from the Russians in the 1860s.

At the time he arrived at the Missouri River for the beginning of RAGBRAI 2000 he hadn't yet selected a name
for this adventure. But with the killing in Shenandoah it
was as if the name picked him. For the July bike ride he
would be "Pat Ripley," a combination of the first name of
his favorite mystery writer, Patricia Highsmith, and the last
name of Tom Ripley, the murderer-hero of Highsmith's remarkable series of novels. The Ripley character, as true
mystery buffs know, is virtually unique in the genre: an ur-
bane killer/hero whose exploits are followed through six
books—sort of a serialized account of a serial killer.

The first time Ripley used his new sobriquet was on the
morning after Spurgeon's murder when he struck up a conversation with Jim Wade. As he rode along he overheard
Wade telling someone he was a mystery writer. He waited for
a break in the conversation and chimed in: "Hey, I think I've
read a couple of your books. I'm Pat Ripley from Denver."

Exhibiting no sense of recognition or whimsy at the mention of Ripley's name, Wade attempted a sweaty, awkward
handshake across his bike frame and said, "Glad to finally
meet a real reader. I hope you liked my books. Tell me, what's
your honest opinion of them?"

As was his wont, Ripley lied smoothly: "They were good
reads. I especially liked the intricate plotting and Midwest-
ern color." What he really thought was that Wade's books
were predictable, crammed with brittle dialogue, and lacked
the morbidity essential to a good murder mystery. In short,

they displayed too much Martha Grimes and not enough Patricia Highsmith. Yes, Ripley decided, Wade was a schlock writer.

Ripley initially found Wade's riding partner, Jennie Wyman, much more interesting. During his first RAGBRAI Ripley had spent several passionate nights in a sleeping bag with a young woman who said she was from West Des Moines. Jennie, although a little old for Ripley's tastes, sported a compact body similar to the one he recalled fondly from the earlier RAGBRAI. As he introduced himself he complimented Jennie on her bike, saying that he was impressed by the level of fitness of a woman who could ride that particular model.

She gave him a curious smile and said without much enthusiasm, "You have a nice bike yourself."

It was clear Jennie was not going to fall for one of his lines, so Ripley backed off. He seldom wasted time with women who did not find him immediately attractive. As a matter of fact, Jennie seemed so taken by Wade that she had little interest in anyone else. No accounting for taste, he thought sadly.

That same day Ripley spent some time with Captain America and the Marvelaires. He found them unpretentious and good for a laugh. Hence, he was shocked to learn that Captain America had been gunned down by Lt. Dallas while attempting to assault a priest. The plot thickens, he guessed. It was a pity that Dallas and the police did not know what Captain America had mentioned to Ripley while the two were riding together. But Ripley would rather have the intrigue continue than to help the authorities unravel it.

Shortly after Captain America ventured off on one of his forays for truth and justice, Ripley was buzzed by "Team South Park." This despicable group of riders, much worse than Team Bad Boy, hailed from the Denver suburb that had inspired the obscenity-laced cartoon show and feature-length movie of the same name. Team South Park was made up of computer geeks, some of whom knew Ripley by his real name. Fortunately, they did not recognize him this time. Each of the members of the team was dressed as a character on *South Park*. As Team South Park swooped down on a vulnerable rider, its members would spew out various crudities and then utter one of the few lines that Pat recognized from the show, "Comin' right for us." Then they would speed by laughing. When Ripley saw them streaming down a short hill he stayed his course. But another rider panicked, swerved sharply onto the shoulder of the road, and unleashed his own torrent of vulgarity. For aesthetic and personal reasons, Pat did not want anything to do with Team South Park.

Curiously, the person with whom Ripley hit it off best on this RAGBRAI was Lars Loving. A liar can usually spot another liar. There was something that did not ring true about Loving. Here was this athletic, savvy guy who was, nonetheless, riding a starter bike and wearing the most garish, non-novelty outfit on RAGBRAI. Loving had first spoken to Ripley on the ride out of Grinnell. Inevitably they got talking about the violence of the previous night. Ripley mainly listened. And he did not volunteer what he knew about the Spurgeon killing or what Captain America had told him. Loving eventually turned the conversation to other topics. "Where are you from, Pat?"

When Loving learned that Ripley was from Denver, they talked for a few minutes about Colorado staples: the Broncos, skiing, and mountain biking. Ripley was a sports fanatic and could discourse for hours about the Broncos' prospects sans Elway, the extra distance a balata-covered golf ball travels in the rarified air at Castle Pines, or the comparative qualities of the black diamond runs at Vail and Winter Park. But, when it became clear that Loving could only handle entry-level sportspeak, they switched topics.

Loving had noticed the special case Ripley had on his bike. "What've you got in there, Pat?"

Ripley proceeded to give him the short version of his story: "It's a laptop. I keep in touch with my customers by e-mail, even this week." In order to maintain conversational parity, Ripley asked, "Lars, what do you do when you're not riding your Huffy?"

Loving joked, "I take a spin in my Jag." Sensing tension creeping in to the conversation, Ripley withdrew into silence. Why was Loving so interested in him? And why did Loving volunteer so little about himself? Ripley took stock. Here was this muscular guy in a tacky green and yellow outfit who sought him out. He didn't know much about sports. He seemed real curious about Ripley's work and leisure activities. And not once in the two hours or so that they had ridden together had he commented on the anatomy or attire of any of the women who sped past them on their nifty ultralight bikes. It could only be one thing: Loving was gay and he was coming on to Ripley.

This realization caused Ripley to regret opening up at all to Loving. Intellectually Ripley had nothing against gays. He had, after all, been against Amendment 2—the Colorado proposition that sought to withdraw state legal protection for the rights of homosexuals. He was pretty sure some of the young guys he hired were gay, and that didn't bother him. But this was personal. It's a good thing, he thought, that most of the details of his life he had offered to Loving had been fabrications. It would not do for Loving or one of his gay friends to come looking for Ripley in Denver. If nothing else, it could put a crimp in his social life.

So Ripley decided to ditch Loving. A couple of miles from Marengo, a town on the western edge of the Amana Colonies, Ripley said, "Lars, I need to take a leak. Ride on ahead; I'll catch up in a mile or so."

Ripley had no intention of meeting up with Loving again. After relieving himself (he really did have to go), he came out of the woods and got back on his bike. No Loving, thank God. He would take it easy for a while until, maybe, Loving would get the message.

After he got back on the road he discovered he was only a few miles from the Amana Colonies Golf Course, one of the fine new golf courses in the Hawkeye State. Although he didn't have his sticks with him, Ripley considered taking a look at the layout. As he was stopped at a lemonade stand debating whether to detour the few miles to the course, a group of riders skidded to a halt. Among them were Jim Wade and Jennie Wyman. Wade and Jennie both recognized Ripley. Jennie was as reluctant to talk to Ripley as she had been on first meeting. Wade, though, hailed Ripley like a long lost brother with a boisterous, "Greetings and felicitations, gentle reader/rider." He then proceed to launch into a monologue about the new RAGBRAI killings. After regaling Ripley with his theories about serial killers and copycat killers, Wade remembered that he had not introduced the other female rider in their three-some.

"Pat," he said, "meet Charlie Andropolous. Charlie owns a bed and breakfast in Bella and occasionally writes for the *Register*. She's also the leader of Team Bella."

Ripley and Charlie shook hands. Although Charlie was perky and friendly, she was not really Ripley's type. So he didn't compliment her on her bike. Charlie noticed Ripley's carrying case and asked about it. He obligingly unfastened the straps and pulled out his computer. "Oooh, that looks like a fine laptop," she said. "I wish the *Register* could spring for one of those for me."

"Well," Ripley responded, "if you get an exclusive on these RAGBRAI killings, I'm sure the paper will grant your wish."

Charlie let out a lively laugh, brushing lightly against Ripley's arm in her exuberance. She did have a nice smile and seemed friendly enough. Maybe, Ripley thought, he had been too hasty in dismissing her.

Before Ripley and Charlie could continue their bantering, Jim Wade said, "Hey, I've got an idea. We've been riding today for what, 50 miles? The day is still young and I'm hungry. There's a great place to eat in Homestead called Bill Zuber's. It's sort of a shrine to Zuber's career as a journeyman baseball player, and the food, in my opinion, is every bit as good there as at the Ronnenburg or the Ox Yoke Inn in Main Amana. I know it's off the official RAGBRAI route a few miles but what the heck."

Charlie chimed in, "Oh that's a great idea. I think I read somewhere that Zuber's would be open during daylight hours today for riders who wanted to make the detour. In fact, if we went to Homestead, took a break for a good meal, and then got back on the regular route to Cedar Rapids, we could probably lay claim to a century day. I need to get away from my team anyway for a couple of hours."

Being a sports fan and starving, Ripley liked the idea of a pilgrimage to Zuber's. Jennie even appeared to warm up to the prospect of a good sit-down meal. So it was unanimous.

The ride on the back roads from South Amana to Homestead was especially pleasant. There was a nice breeze from the west that pushed the foursome smoothly past the beautifully groomed fields. As they moved off the official RAGBRAI route the crowds of riders peeled away and they had the road to themselves. To make conversation Ripley asked, "What are these Amana Colonies, anyway?"

Charlie and Wade, both proud Iowans, tried to enlighten Ripley. But all he got out of their history lesson was that the

Amanas were German communal villages and "weren't
Amish." Arriving in Homestead about 1:30, they found
Zuber's easily and were delighted to discover they had the
place almost to themselves. Ripley learned from the memo-
rabilia scattered throughout the small restaurant that Bill
"Goober" Zuber had indeed played major league baseball. He
had pitched for four American League teams in the thirties
and forties, compiling a record of 43 wins and 42 losses. He
filed this trivia away, hoping to be able to dredge it up sometime in the future to impress his buddies back in Colorado.

Ripley and the others indulged themselves in large por-
tions of Amana ham, bratwurst, Wiener schnitzel and all
the wonderful German side dishes. No one worried about
calories on RAGBRAI, but this meal pushed the envelope.
The prospect of a homemade dessert beckoned, but the pitcher
of iced tea Ripley had drunk compelled him first to seek out
the restroom. A few minutes later, on his way to the table,
he happened to glance out a window. Outside the restaurant by a quaint picket fence was Lars Loving, of all people.
He was talking to Lt. Dallas. What were they doing so far off
the RAGBRAI route? And what did this fruity-colored rider
have to say to the Commander of the Iowa State Patrol?

As Ripley pondered the possiblities, Loving pointed to
the four bikes parked outside Zuber's. Both Loving and Dallas
then started walking toward the restaurant. As Ripley continued to stare at the two men, Loving caught sight of him
in the window and waved. His gesture seemed friendly
enough, but Ripley didn't know what to make of Loving's

sly smile. However, it was the nasty expression on Dallas's face that really bothered him. Ripley suddenly lost his appetite for raspberry pie a la mode.

JOHN JOHNSON *is the Head of the Department of History at the University of Northern Iowa where he teaches courses in U.S. history and historical methods. His most recent book is* The Struggle for Student Rights: Tinker v. Des Moines and the 1960s *(University Press of Kansas, 1997) which was an Honorable Mention recipient of the Benjamin F. Shambaugh Award which recognizes outstanding books on Iowa history. He is currently preparing the second edition of a reference work,* Historic U.S. Court Cases: An Encyclopedia *(Garland Publishing, forthcoming 2001) which won the Thomas Jefferson Award of the Society for History in Federal Government as the outstanding reference source on the history of the federal government for 1992 and 1993. John was born, raised, and educated in Minnesota. He and his family currently reside in Cedar Falls. Prior to coming to Iowa in 1988, he lived in New York and South Carolina. John hasn't ridden a bike in years, but he likes Patricia Highsmith novels and has been known to play an occasional round of golf.*

13
Derailleur

By Kathleen A. Kelly

Charlie leaned into her handlebars, into the dry prairie wind. Her legs and thighs hurt, burned by the afternoon sun. Her skin only burned like this once before; Tim Sturgeon's hands had been soft and his words a whisper, tracing the whitened scar left from the surgeon's scalpel. She lowered her eyes, focusing on Highway 6 and her cycling trek across Iowa.

Her youth was disappearing; her chestnut hair now faded nutmeg or cinnamon. She felt herself beginning to fade—her dreams no longer grandiose and her illusions all but dead alongside the corpse of her calico cat when she was six, the first of too many corpses . . . and now one more.

"So, have you written about the murder for the *Register?*" Lars Loving inquired. "I haven't read any of your articles. What do you make of those knife wounds and the plucked-out eyes? Pretty sick people out there. Creepy, when you really think about it. I just hope the police can catch this guy. But with 16,000 suspects, it's tough, you know. What do you think?"

When I took him to our family farm, I never showed him the cat's grave but turned to him with an open embrace and cried for all the grace that nothing like what happened to my cat should ever happen to him. His eyes, once blue topaz, at the end looked tired, pale like aquamarine water turned murky in a lake contaminated by all its visitors. He rested in the icy snow, white wind of the prairie, saying goodbye to the land my father toiled for years, turning fallow ground into rows of golden corn and clovered hay sprinkled with the violet of thistles and flower. He could only see the sky above him and hear the distant ringing of the bells bidding him farewell.

"I didn't know I'd be riding this year; it was a last minute thing. If I had known, I would be riding my Trek, burning up the road. This Huffy, what a piece of well, you know, mierde. And would you look at this green and gold; I'm not even a Packers fan."

"Really?" she responded, hoping that he would stop talking, that she could enjoy some silence.

She had been anxious, lonely after Ken returned to Japan to edit his documentary film about America's not so peaceful or provincial heartland. She walked around the rooms at the Three Sisters Bed and Breakfast trying to keep busy and directed, intent on her emerging writing career. As time went on, she began to worry every time she left the inn that she had forgotten something: had she left the doors unlocked, the candles burning, the oven burners on, the bath water running? The silence became deafening, unbearable. She forced herself to find new material.

She would go to the Whiskey Grove in Bella where she would read James Joyce's "The Dead" and drink Shirley Temples with extra cherries. "Welcome to the Jungle" was the musical staple of most evenings and she began from square one, sketching the settings and people. Hours, days and evenings blurred together and she could no longer hear anything but the low buzz of bar philosophies, droning like the sea of locusts before their landing along the Nile, liberating the Hebrews from their servitude.

"Miss, would you like another drink?" the bartender asked between sips of whiskey and a beer chaser. He waited for her answer, staring at her St. Christopher's medallion, watching the strained movement of her lips, twitching as though her decision on this drink would change the course of her life. She sat mute.

"If you need another, just let me know . . . " and he walked away, tucking his bar rag into the slouched pocket of his faded Levi's, bouncing in his high top Chuck Taylors, oblivious to the ways of the world. He rounded the bar and played pool.

Tim Sturgeon had been silent in his approach. He asked, "Do you have a cigarette?" She stared ahead, at his reflection in the mirror.

"You know," he said, "I've never lit a woman's cigarette in my life." He gave her a cigarette from his pack and lit it with his embossed lighter, his initials TS shining, reflected in the dark, smoky light. He told her everything and nothing, and taught her that the best love was both intimate and distant. After leaving, he'd call her from time to time or send her notes from Bangkok, Hong Kong, scratch rubbings from the Lil Qala and Red Palace.

"Querida, distance yourself from me. I can't call you anymore. It's not safe for you. Just trust me on this one."

Joliet Prison declared his death an accident, unsolved causes that they would continue to investigate. Her investigation let her to her own conclusions: members of racketeering and extortion fronted at the Joliet prison.

"Earth to Charlie, come in, Charlie." She turned to her right and smiled at her blond companion. "You were a million miles away. Welcome back to the land of the living."

"Worlds away." She felt the burn again, continued to pedal, hoping to feel alive again.

She felt nothing. Tim Sturgeon . . . Tom Spurgeon. Had he been alive, and was he now really dead? During her Tarot reading last night she asked for help, direction. In the seventh card position, was the Hanged Man, represented by Odin. According to Teutonic legend, Odin volunteered his own sacrifice and rejuvenation. Wounded by his own spear, he remained hanging from the tree, shaken by a powerful wind. No one came to Odin; no one helped him. He extended his hands toward some runes, picked one up and was immediately released from his position by their worldly magic.

Lars touched his gloved hand to her shoulder, "I'm so glad that we lost the others, that we've shared this leg of the ride together."

She nodded, pedaling even harder, faster.

"I've become lazy here. I know that you won't believe it but I was in awesome shape while at the Academy in Quantico. This Huffy really doesn't help my performance either."

His voice became the droning of locusts, chewing away at the flesh. Her head was throbbing. Temperatures were hovering near 100 and she began to see mirages, camels and bedouins in the desert.

"I can't believe how well this bike has held up especially since I'm not very good at maintenance—or anything else technical for that matter. Hell, I'm still trying to figure out how to e-mail and dial out on my cell phone."

She laughed, aware that his false humility was supposed to solicit such a response. Time, chance, and one wrong move, one slight shift can turn your world upside-down. One minute, the next minute, a few minutes later, and then a year, a decade, centuries.

"Hope Jennie's OK after her talk with Lt. Dallas. Maybe I should stop and call and see if we can meet them in Cedar rapids. Do you know what her cell number is?"

"Eight, six, seven, five, three, Oh, nine."

"Blah, blah, blah," he continued.

"Uh, huh."

"Blah, blah, blah."

Charlie continued to climb up the slight incline, heard the rustling leaves of sweet corn and felt small pelts of rain. Lars stopped to call, then packed his cell phone away and set out on his Huffy again, shifting gears. Desperately sprinting after her, his chain caught and he flipped head first onto the wet pavement. He only heard the sound of the approaching Mack truck before he fainted.

Rain pelted her face, her bangs flattened to her forehead. She knew that no runes in the world could save him. It was an accident; she did not mean to harm him.

KATHLEEN A. KELLY *earned a Master's Degree in History from the University of Northern Iowa in 1991. She has published articles, book reviews, interviews, and poetry in* Al-Jadid, Amelia, Astrophysicist's Tango Partner Speaks, Calyx, Clean Sheets, Factsheet 5, Green Hills Literary Lantern, The Iowan, Litspeak, Rain Taxi Teaching for Success, *and other publications. A former grantee of the National Endowment for the Humanities and college instructor at Northeast Iowa Community college—Peosta. She is now studying for her master of Fine Arts degree in poetry at Eastern Washington University at Spokane where she works at the university press and as a freelance writer/editor. Kathleen wishes to thank John Rogerson for his help with this chapter.*

14
The Pearl-Handled Kill

By Stephen Pett

Lars Loving, mumbling in a coma: NO! No no nobody knows the trouble I've never been so light light opens like a tent burning mornings I think today burning eight how did the Buddha say zen so close my fist around a handlebar bursting bone-handled knives my father said a man's outsides reflect his inside mine six her house we drank Pepsis and she let me kiss her that first time with mouths open and she said you got the right name you I said the first time seven I chased down a stranger armed only with freeze I said stop that this minute my mother said you can't bring a pistol five into this guy's dressed like the flag Evel Knievel on steroids Jesus the tongues and eyes the bore boring from the bore of a pistol but wait blades wait sharp wait until the cameraman's ready she said three dead Angi's mouth holding light on lips saying you she said you're Tom Cruise kiss me Tom Cruise the early Tom the latest bloody sad Angie said I'm too old without wind is all this is I can do fifty pushups with one arm but my arm folds oh my fist opens yes light firelight burning tented out of flames pearly fingered a ringing my father milk a milkman rang a bell bottles rang against one another broke like blades her eyes black-patched over the final the teacher asked what is a criminal he she looked at me nine to see eyes burning if I'd live yes I said yes yes

Recorded by Lieutenant Scott Dallas:

Wasn't nothing reckless about it. You want reckless put ten thousand monkeys on bicycles, man. I been hearing about the murders all the way from Rapid. Reckless woulda been me vaporizing the dude. Wasn't for nothing I took first place in the truck driver rodeo three weeks back. Sixteen wheels, man. In Ames. I got a trophy. Ok. I made a little booboo cutting over here, a shortcut a buddy told me about. But reckless I wasn't. I was crawling at the time. I am the master of this machine. You understand? Here's how I told it to my grandma. I says, "Our people mastered the horse until the horse's day was done. Me, my truck's my prairie pony."

"You ain't no Crazy Horse," she says. "Got a dog on the front."

"Dogs can bite," I says.

"The dust," she says. "I'm praying for you."

Ok maybe it's her prayers saved the dude. But I've got the skill. My wipers are flappin', Tom T. Hall on the box, he goes down and in the blink of an eye I cut the wheel and

I'm into that field there then back on the road. Even though the ground's wet, man. You try it. I didn't drive him off, the other way around. Ask him, he's comin' around.

He couldn't been out more than a minute. I run back and I'm leaning over him when he opens his eyes. The word "yes" kind of hisses out of him while his eyeballs are rolling slow in his face. Then with a quick breath in between each number he says—hell, I even wrote it down— eight, six, seven, five, three, oh, nine. Does that twice, and all the time that lady, well you can see, she's out of her damn head, carrying on about Joliet, I know what that is, how he's dead, and I can't listen cause I'm trying to see if the guy's hurt bad, even though he's smiling. I guess you could call that dopey grin a smile. His hand's all torn up but he's flashing those teeth.

Course by then the cavalry come, bike riders bunched around us, with every damn one, it seemed, jabbering into a cell phone. Guess that's how you got here so quick. What a world.

How about this one? I've dragged him loose of his bicycle and when I get the bike out of the road I see what it is. One of them Huffies—the people's bike—but here's what I read on the crossbar, the model: Lakota. I tell you there was nothing reckless in any of this. Fate, brother, fate.

Fate. Five hours earlier, Lars Loving pedaled east, beside a man he believed he knew. The wind poured over them, gritty at times, but thick with a field sweetness, a sweetness Lars remembered from his Aunt's place near Ladora, another memory he tried to ignore. He had a job. Now he had a duty: a pact he made with himself. He was an investigator—a trained investigator. He shifted and for a moment his derailieur caught and Pat Ripley pumped ahead.

Pat Ripley. The guy looked like he should have Mattel stamped on his back. Stiff, that was the thing about him. Not stiff in the way he moved. He flew over the small hills. Stiff in the way he let whatever was inside out. The line of his mouth never changed. He didn't turn his head to look at you; he rotated it. Then how about the eyes, what Lars's old criminology professor called "the portals of truth"? Ripley's eyes—the one time Loving saw them without the black Oakleys—could have been made of wax, smooth blue wax. His voice punched words out of tin, deflected questions: "Feel like I'm on the moon. You come down from the mile-high, you cheat physiology for a spell. Pretend I'm John Elway for a day or two." A laugh like a cat coughing. The face from the movies. That's what Angi had said.

Angi Gales. Strolled up to him where he sat leaning against an oak down past the softball field at the edge of Heritage Park in Grinnell. She said, "Hey, I thought I saw you headed this way." The cicadas whirred through the deepening dark, over the music, the laughter, people relaxed, unwinding, forgetting themselves. Lars started to stand. "No," she said, "I'd like to sit, if you don't mind." She pressed her fingertips to his arm. "I just finished making an ass of myself. That and well, I'm worried about my friend."

She crossed her legs so that their knees nearly touched. Her breath smelled like strawberries, and she breathed over him as she talked. "It's not that she's hooked up with this mystery writer, I'm really glad for her, even though he's like this big spooky mystery himself, it's how she's, well, gotten all edgy since that, you know, that sick-weird killing. It's made us all edgy, I guess, but you're a cop, you knew Jennie from classes or something, you must have instincts."

"It's more than instinct," Lars said. "But without that, nothing else counts."

"Well, I've got my instincts. And they tell me; Angi, Jennie Wyman is in deep—"

"We know about Spurgeon, we know about Jennie."

"No. Listen, did anybody ever tell you you look like Tom Cruise, the young Tom Cruise, before he looked like he wears a toupee? I need to talk it out."

"Angi." In the glow from the center of the park, her cheek gleamed, and her lips caught the light, a small sliver of gold, and how old was she, and he should keep his mind on duty. Duty. "All right, but I'm no priest."

She jumped.

He leaned forward, and now he pressed his fingertips to her arm. "I'm no shrink either. Just a pair of willing ears."

"You're a cop. This is for a cop. Lars—"

"Get it off your chest."

"That night, that awful night, there's a rock under my sleeping bag, or a root. Anyway I toss and turn, and finally I get up to double-check I'd locked my bike. No Jennie. Ok,

I think, she's a big girl, she can fend for herself. Probably being romantic in the bushes somewhere. I'd seen her with Wade. And then I thought, this is you, Angi Gales, foot-loose, ready to absorb, to soak up experience. Like a pilgrim or something. Well my bike's locked tight, of course, and I laugh at myself, and I walk. A makeshift community of friendly strangers, a sky thinning out with the sun getting close under a gazillion stars."

"Slow down," Lars said. "It's okay."

She took his hand. Her eyes shined. "I'm, well, I'm walking down by the creek, it must be tree frogs that chirp like that, and somebody sprints by then stumbles and it's dark still but not, you know, and I'd swear it's Jennie. Not like a scared run, but hurrying. I'm curious, of course, so I walk up this little slope into these trees where a couple of tents are pitched. I hear a dog whimpering, real low, and this guy, straight as a tree, is just standing there, arms at his side. Talk about creepy. Whew. Like . . . Who's that guy in all the horror movies?"

"Christopher Walken."

"Yeah, you read my mind. Like him. And I don't even know if he saw me, but as I'm backing away, he squeaks out this little series of laughs, like a cat coughing." Her arm trembled under Lars' hand. Her voice trembled. Or was it Lars, some shaking in his center rippling out. She said, "I'm backing off, then, I'm walking fast and looking back, and what I saw was what you can guess I saw. That tent. Holy moly. It's on fire."

They hugged each other then, fire where their skin touched. Fire in the sound of those million bugs grinding, the music pounding, the frogs here, too. Frogs and fire. Her lips met his neck and a blowtorch scorched up his spine. He gripped her shoulders, held her back. "The guy, the Christopher Walken guy. Have you seen him since?"

"Oh yeah." The words came close beside his ear. "I'll bet you've noticed him, even out of these thousands, even with all the costumes and craziness, he's like the weirdest. His bike's gold, with honking big shocks on the front. He's got this laptop he hauls along, says it's to e-mail 'clients.' All I've seen him do is play Doom." She said the word again, holding out the *oo* across his cheek, his ear. He lightly laid his hand against her ear, as he allowed their mouths to meet, to open. Strawberries. And his other hand moved up her back, with the bugs grinding, with her hand, fingers spread, slowly sliding a circle on his shoulder. "Oh." Which of them made the sound?

The jolt went through them. A scream. Another. Close. A couple of hundred yards.

"Lars, please," she said, as he jumped up. "I need—"

"Duty," he said. "I'm sorry. I am truly, truly sorry." He bent and kissed the top of her head, her smoky hair, and sprinted into an even noisier darkness.

And if he hadn't left?

He couldn't shake it. No way should he blame himself. He heard screams, he's a trained law enforcement officer, he runs. Nothing she said would have told anyone she was in immediate danger. Right? He left her, that was the truth of the deal, a woman alone in a park full of lurking intentions. Lars now knew he would crack this thing. Absolutely. No way should he blame himself, but he owed her. When he heard who had been killed, when he heard how, he stood off by himself. He could not accompany Dallas to see the corpse. He stood off by himself and made a vow, "Whoever you are, I'll hunt you down. You'll look at me, me on my Huffy, in my silly damn outfit, and you will not suspect that I am your fate."

"I am your fate," he wanted to say to Pat Ripley as they rode. "What you know I will know. She was beautiful."

"Lars," Ripley called, "I need to take a leak. Ride on ahead; I'll catch up in a mile or so."

So Lars did, because what else could he do? Ripley clearly was master of his own surface, could not be rattled on the road, on this straight course with everyone hunched, pedaling, rolling as though they were all the same, as though they each meant no harm, meant only to ride this road to a happy ending. No happy endings for Angi.

When he was a kid at his aunt's place in Ladora, Lars drowned a chicken. Aunt Sadie said the chicken was sick and needed to be "put out of its misery." She gave him an old rusty hatchet, but how could he bring the blade down on its neck. So he decided to hold it under the surface of the water in the old barrel. It flapped underwater. How he felt then was how he felt now, a cold sour putty in his stomach. He could almost imagine he saw that place in Ladora from here. Almost imagine he could walk into that stand of sun-flowers and coneflowers where Aunt Sadie took him after the chicken, after he calmed down some. She said, "There's death in the scheme of the universe, Lars. You didn't invent it, and you can't make it pretty."

"You can't make it pretty," Lars said to himself now, pumping faster and faster away from Pat Ripley, faster into the grit, the sweetness, a world so wide you should never be able to fall off. "You can't make it pretty," he said to himself. "But you can try to make it right." Past the South Park crowd, women with wings, families towing yellow carts with orange flags, and TV people, people, people. You'd think the murders would drive them off, but no, the murders seemed to pull people in. Pumping. Until he saw, what? A police cruiser out there in the middle of all this, off on the shoulder. And slumped inside, hands folded over the steering wheel, Lt. Scott Dallas, whom he had hoped to see, wanted to catch alone since the nightmare of last night.

"Sir," Lars said, opening the passenger side. The car sweltered.

"Loving," Lt. Dallas said. Sweat streaked his face.

"Sir," Lars said, lifting his legs inside. "I hope I'm not sticking my nose in, but, sir, you don't look so good. Maybe we ought to step outside. You know, maybe we should get out of the car, get some air. Sir!"

Lt. Dallas's eyes snapped. His shoulders straightened. "Yes," he said.

They walked slowly in foxtails up to their knees, and the

lieutenant was breathing evenly now. The color rose though his cheeks, but he chewed his lip. "It's getting to me, Loving. I won't lie to you. Two more died last night. Two people I failed. God, I killed a guy dressed like a damn comic book, shot him. I'll level with you, Lars. It sure as hell looked like he was going to kill that priest, Sure as hell. But now . . . Hindsight's—"

"I could have saved the Gale woman."

Lt. Dallas spit. "You and the marines."

"I was with her. She was scared, bad scared, and when I heard a scream, I took off and left her."

"We're like rent-a-cops, you know? Jesus. All uniform and no mustard."

Lars took the Lieutenant's arm. "You got the mustard, Lieutenant. We can't quit. That's what we owe the dead. Angi Gales, she told me something I've been wanting to tell you ever since. No chance."

And so, after asking half a dozen riders, and making two calls, the last to this place they were now pulling up to, Bill Zuber's in Homestead, Lars Loving and Lieutenant Dallas understood one another. More importantly, they had come to understand the past few days' events in ways neither could have alone. Lars unloaded the Huffy from the trunk, locked it to an antique green water pump, and walked with Lt. Dallas up the walk. He saw Ripley through the window as jays made a racket from the trees, and he waved, his teeth grinding.

"Need to ask a few questions," Lieutenant Dallas said, after Jim Wade invited them to sit down, join them for pie.

Portals of truth, Lars thought, but he couldn't read their eyes, and Ripley wore his shades. "Start with you, if you don't mind, Mr. . . . Ripley, is it?" Ripley pushed back his chair, rose stiffly.

Jennie Wyman stood too, brushed the hair from her cheeks, and said, "Lars, Lars, could I have a word with you in . . . in private?" Now Lars noticed eyes registering, two in particular, those of Jim Wade, eyes darting from Jennie to his plate to the cruiser outside.

"Go ahead, Lars," Lieutenant Dallas said. Dallas and Ripley followed Lars and Jennie Wyman back out of the air-conditioning and the thick smell of ham. Dallas led Ripley down a brick path, Ripley taking one measured step on those plastic legs after another.

Jennie leaned against the cruiser, dropped a backpack from her shoulder to the gravel. They had often studied for criminology exams together, his idea since she seemed to get concepts before anyone else. She'd helped him over maybe five different evenings, and never once, he realized now, had she ever revealed anything personal. She squinted up at him, so that lines spread through her skin, almost like glass breaking.

"Loving," she said, very softly. No hint of nervousness— or grief. "You're a straight arrow, too straight for the rest of us, you ask me. But I'm counting on that in you. I just lost a friend, a good friend, an old friend. What I am right now is frightened big time." The eyes said otherwise. They glanced over her shoulder at the big window of Bill Zuber's. She stooped and reached into her pack. What she pulled out was a book. On its creased cover was the shadowy figure of a man, a man above the body of a blonde woman in a red dress. *The Blunt Instrument,* by James Wade, "another Blade Harkin mystery."

"Read it," Jennie said. "That's all I can say. You'll understand."

Lars wanted to ask about Angi, that night the tent burned, but just then Charlie Andropolous rushed from Bill Zuber's.

"I'm going," she said. "I want to get there. I'm going." She pushed past Lars.

Lars said, "Jennie, level with me. You have a cell phone, don't you."

The eyes said nothing. "A phone. I . . . I borrowed one yesterday or the day before—"

"Loving," Lt. Dallas interrupted. "That woman. She shouldn't be riding alone. And . . . you know."

Lars did know, so he stuffed the book in his fanny pack and swung aboard his trusty Huffy to accompany Charlie Andropolous.

And now here he was sore all over on a soft bed in Cedar Rapids, his hand bandaged, his head throbbing—when any cop worth his salt would be out investigating, when any man worth his salt would be hunting down Angi Gales's killer. He wanted to thank the driver of the truck, who had said, "It's a bad day to die." Zenith would interrogate that whacked-out Charlie Andropolous. And Lars had held onto the cell-phone number. Resting was in the interest of his pact, Lars knew. Also, Lt. Dallas said, "We have to put our heads together tonight. We're close. Do your research."

This was Lieutenant Dallas's sister's house—her children were with their father this summer—and Lars could hear her puttering downstairs. She hugged him when they met. She looked like Shania Twain with red hair and maybe twenty pounds. Another woman alone. She fluffed his pillow, but then she saw the cover of his book and laughed. "Are you hooked on those?"

Lars mumbled, finally said, "Part of this case we're on."

"Couldn't be much of a case," she said. "That man's got one plot. The killer's always, and I mean always, been wronged in love and is missing a body part, ear, nose . . . Oh yeah, and the knives."

With that she pulled his door shut, and Lars, even with his eyes hurting the way they did, opened the book and started chapter one, "The Pearl-Handled Kill."

STEPHEN PETT *is a member of the Creative Writing faculty at Iowa State University. He is the author of* Sirens, *a novel, and* Pulpit of Bones, *a collection of poetry. His short stories are widely published and have been cited in* Best American Short Stories *and syndicated by Fiction Network. He is the founding Editor of* Flyway, *a literary magazine. On leave from ISU the past two years, he taught 11th and 12th grade English at the Native American Preparatory School in Rowe, New Mexico.*

15

"Tell Me More, Tell Me More."

By Grant Tracey

Father Mike O'Connor was enjoying the bass groove, a heavy downbeat with a bright counterpoint, as he awkwardly danced on the terrace of the Old Capitol Building in Iowa City. His arms jerked like acute-angled oil derricks as the glim dim light from the dome shone across the terrace balustrade. Behind him slumped a banner that looked like faded basketball twine. "Welcome RAGBRAI Riders. Let's Party Down!"

Jennie Wyman, her hair no longer pulled back in a long rope but now dangling like Cleopatra, jerked and hopped across from Father Mike, the red and blue arcs of the propped kleig lights cutting her face into a Picasso painting where nothing seemed to match up. And then she threw back her narrow shoulders and shouted in her best Olivia Newton John manner.

Father O'Connor, on the other hand, deliberately muffed some of the more racy lines, like "Down in the sand," and then the crowd, a haze of colors, some still in helmets that glowed like a series of interconnecting lakes, slugged the chorus in a raunchy grind-house way, "Tell me more, Tell me more."

The Father found himself blushing a little for being up on stage and doing karaoke. He wasn't really an outgoing type, but he had won the Bill Clinton look-a-like contest and Jennie was "Monica" so they had to do this honorary dance. Actually, the young Father knew their winning was a lie, a small corruption, a moment of rationalization within an irrational design, because he had asked Jill Stewart, the event's organizer in Iowa City and a former student at Seminary, to pick him and Jennie. After all, he was Irish and looked a little like the president, and Jennie, with her sassy new big hair, could pass for a slimmer Monica, sort of, but the truth was he really needed to talk to her, and this ruse maybe would give him the chance. There was a lot Captain America had confessed that Father O'Connor hadn't told the police.

Father O'Connor danced some more steps that he knew made him look like a hockey player avoiding a crosscheck, but he shrugged at Jennie sheepishly and kept jumping as if cut glass were all around his feet. Periodically he'd glance behind, down Madison Street and Hubbard Park to the Iowa river. He could barely see it through the red brick buildings and haze of night, but he knew it was high and in the glints of moonlight imagined black lines forming that looked like curving snakes. It had rained a lot in July, and last night a downpour swelled the river to flood levels. Earlier in the day volunteers had stacked the shores with white sand bags that looked like the strung beads of a rosary.

But it wasn't the weather that forced Team Fatherhood, O'Connor's fellow priests, to leave at midday Friday for Dubuque. They had services to attend to, but the young priest decided to stay on at Iowa City, against their wishes, to pursue truth. A few years back, when he was fresh out of seminary, Father O'Connor had found himself enjoying confession a little too much. The stories of others' transgressions filled him with pain and empathy, but also interested him in ways that didn't seem appropriate. He related these feelings to several of his fellow priests and they told him his thoughts were sinful: his purpose was to absolve sin, not to find "intrigue" in it. He asked for forgiveness, but also tried to clarify his feelings. It wasn't that he enjoyed sin, but that he found himself wanting to lose his innocence in the experiences of others. Exploring those experiences made him feel as if he were prying, and there were risks involved in gaining such knowledge.

The crowd jumped and sang to more lyrics, and their dome-shaped tents seemed to jump too, and then Jennie dropped to her knees during the song's final "Tell me more" crescendo. The priest grinned at her slightly and then looked back at the tents spread across a banner of grass.

Jill held up their hands. Her fingers felt damp and trembled slightly. "Let's hear it for Bill and Monica!"

As the crowd cheered, Father O'Connor abruptly backed away, and then he and Jennie walked down the terrace. A middle-aged man, his hair slicked with sweat, clutched Jennie's wrist as they reached a final curve by the grass's edge. He suggested they grab some funnel cakes by vendor's row near MacBride Hall. He wasn't really asking; it was more of an order.

"Uh, Jennie? I need to talk to you. It won't take long," the Father interrupted.

"It's okay, Jim," she said looking at her partner. Their eyes seemed to dance through shoulders and were afraid to look on each other. "It's okay." She took a white towel from him and wiped her hair. "That was fun," she said to the Father. "I didn't know that priests could dance. I mean, would want to dance. Jim, it's okay. It'll only take a few minutes." She patted Jim twice on the hips, and he said he'd get some funnel cakes and meet her back in his tent.

Jennie and the Father walked down the dip in the capitol lawn, and passed several tents. On the terrace, new karaoke seekers were singing "Paradise by the Dashboard Light," while across the street, the Father could make out the red and white gleam of Danforth Chapel. In front of it was an emergency phone booth that looked like a blue-filtered ciga- rette. "It was fun," he said, to break the silence, and then he abashedly confessed. "Actually, it wasn't really a surprise. I asked Jill. I know her. I asked her to pick us."

Jennie paused, her left hand on her hip, her right eye- brow arched like the back of a cat. "What's this all about,

Father?"

"Are you Catholic, Jennie?"

"On my mother's side."

"Not that it matters." He looked away. On the crests of the rushing river, light sparkled like flecks of fireflies in a dirty jar. "Did you kill Tom Spurgeon?"

Lt. Scott Dallas squinted his lean eyes as he propped against his police cruiser parked in front of the old Capitol building. Two photographs were scattered on the hood of his car. Next to him stood a wobbly Lars Loving, a bandage wrapped loosely around his head like a white tornado. "Then tell me. Who the hell is Captain America?"

On the other side of the park, someone was singing something or other about fighting authority and winning. Lt. Dallas smirked over such false celebrations of freedom.

"The original's Jim Edgars. The guy you killed is somebody else," Dr. Strange of the Marvelaires said, throwing his cape over his left shoulder. Next to him ran a low flung fence that looked like oversized cribbage pegs connected with black lace.

"Yeah," Thor said. He was twice the size of Lars Loving and was leaning on his Villisca ax. "That's not Jim."

Lt. Dallas studied the photographs of the dead guy once more, and then passed them to Lars. "Lars. You getting all this? So, Thor, you're telling me that this dead guy, this serial killer, the Eye Doctor, is not the Captain America you guys usually ride with. Here and in San Francisco and all that?"

"Yes, that's right. It's not Jim," Spidey said, some of his cross-stitched webbing looking crooked in spots.

And then Lt. Dallas felt a sharp tingle in his eyes and cheeks, a tingle that was more like a carpet burn. Did he kill a serial killer or someone pretending to be one? Was the real killer still loose? Was Edgars the real killer? Was Edgars dead, another victim, and then this whack job used his costume to take out Angi Gales or Kristen Jensen—or both?

"It's freaking us out, man," Thor said.

Lt. Dallas looked at Thor's ax and tried to suppress a laugh, but he felt a crooked squiggle tremor through his lips. "So tell me about Jim."

Jim Edgars, the original Cap, according to Dr. Strange, was a farm kid from Red Oak who attended the University of Nebraska and always wore Sooners sweatshirts just to piss everybody off. He eventually got a Master's degree in business and did a lot of online selling and buying. He often went to Denver and Chicago for business trips.

"So when did the switch between the Caps happen, do you think?" Lars asked, tired and bending slightly at the waist, his hands tugging on the crisp ends of his shorts.

"I don't know," Dr. Strange said. His voice was thin and limp like crinkled tissue and didn't fit with his regal look. "But that dead guy in the pictures ain't him."

"I think we've established that, thanks," Lt. Dallas said, tersely. Now the crowd behind the building was shouting about some damn love shack.

"Jim's a practical joker," Spidey said, the reflected panels in his eye holes blinding Lt. Dallas, preventing him from peering in. "And maybe it's all a joke. I mean, he's into jokes." Spidey shrugged as the dim lantern lighting around them cast hexagonal shadows.

"What kind of jokes?" Lars asked, leaning against a huge rock that was engraved with some important class of phoneys or something from "1880."

Spidey started to chuckle, explaining how Jim loved to get online and into various databases and find out who worked at the local Wal-Mart. And then, the next day, dressed like a suit, he would arrive with a bunch of pink slips and give a lot of "working class flunkeys" their two-week notices. "I mean that's a riot."

Lt. Dallas figured Jim was real big on control. "Yeah. That's a real riot."

Jennie stood in back of Danforth Chapel, her shoulders trembling. Behind her ran a railroad track, silver, sprinkled with graffiti that looked like soggy cereal. The tracks crossed the river and a sign read "Warning Turn Back. River Use Restrictions Ahead by City Ordinance." Father O'Connor couldn't look at her; instead, he kept reading the sign.

Jennie, too, said nothing. She had been crying for awhile. She said she had thought of killing Tom because he was stalking her, as he had before. The Father didn't want to think of everything she had said. It was too painful.

"You don't understand, Father. Nobody does."

They walked along the bicycle path toward a tunnel. Faintly the Father could make out the lyrics to "Mack the Knife." The singer's voice mixed with Bobby Darin's to create a smooth milkshake stirred with sun block.

"Don't you see what's happening, Jennie?" She looked at him. Captain America had told him he was supposed to kill Tom. *Supposed.* "Someone hired Captain America. Someone else wanted him dead."

They paused in the tunnel, and the Father, again, glanced at graffiti. Some was chipped away, like "op Violence Against Women," the black-lettered meaning slightly obscured. "Why did somebody else want Tom dead?"

"I don't know." Jennie mentioned Joliet, drugs with prisoners, and the witness protection program, but she said she didn't know anything beyond that.

"What if the real murder hasn't happened yet?"

"Huh?"

They exited the tunnel, and the Father tapped his chin. Jennie played with her pink wrist band. "I know it's just fiction, but, it's an old Agatha Christie trick."

"You read mysteries?"

"Yes, of course. I don't only read the Bible."

She smiled.

"Actually, I used to read a lot of detective stories before I became a priest. And in the mid-eighties, I read a lot of comic books, too. Not Captain America but alternative titles like Cerebus, Alien Worlds, and Ms. Tree. You look a little like her, sort of."

"Ms. Tree?"

"Yes. She was a female Mike Hammer." He kicked at a wedged stone. "No. There actually was a Mike Hammer type and he got killed off and she took over his business. But I digress. Back to Agatha Christie. In her novels, a series of meaningless murders happens to divert the police from the real murder. And in this case all of the diversion surrounds you."

"That seems far-fetched," she said, and Father O'Connor shrugged as a faint spacey-techno song about a love shack filled their silences.

Jennie pressed her lips together. "Why not just say I killed everyone? I put the knives in Tom's eyes to divert suspicion, and then I killed them all? That makes more sense than your diversion theory."

"Maybe. But I don't think you did." He smiled and looked up at the bridge. It was marked with fist-sized holes that looked like sun spots. "But you've got to tell the authorities. Not just to save your soul, but to save your friends' lives. Angi, your roommate, is dead. Kristen, whom you told me about, is also dead. As long as you're silent, the killings will mount. Your friends, contacts, are the targets, the diversion from the real murder. Maybe Jim will be killed next."

"Jim?" Jennie looked down at her blue sneakers stained with dew. "I'm worried that Jim might be the killer. Those mystery stories I told you about? They always have the same plot: dead women and pearl-handled knives."

The priest nodded and looked back at the black lines in

the river. He couldn't understand how a man who wrote such hatred could teach at Wartburg College. And then he also thought of how possessive Jim had been around Jennie just a few minutes ago. Father O'Connor didn't know Jim Wade at all.

"I'm ready to finish my confession now, Father," Jennie said.

The Father turned around, and saw Jennie kneeling by the shore, and at that moment he was struck by Jennie's beauty. It wasn't the beauty of the body, but the beauty of the soul that seemed to shine from within and without and glow like a holy image on stained glass, an image of grace and faith, and the Father felt ashamed for looking on such purity. To look made him wonder if his own pursuit of knowledge were akin to Adam's in the garden and the quest for the apple, and it made him wonder if he were treading where he ought not, if some knowledge ought not to be known, and then he heard a swish, followed by Jennie's stark scream that thudded into his head like black birds breaking over a bridge.

The Father gasped for air and rose above the crest of the river. Then he dropped down and bobbed up again. Wet spots glowed like glass stains on counter tops and he tried to see the shoreline as the current carried him down, down, down. He looked for Jennie and saw a dark shadow of a man, holding a club or a knife, and then more spots, and then along the beads of sand bags, a glint of light, a sharp arc, like an angel's wing.

GRANT TRACEY *teaches film, popular culture, and creative writing at the University of Northern Iowa. His stories and essays have appeared in a variety of venues including* Kansas Quarterly *and* Aethlon: The Journal of Sport Literature. *His hardboiled detective story,* "Moonlit Farewell," *featuring Rockin' Rick Dragon, was the first publication in G. W. Clift's* Twister *Chapbook Series out of Manhattan, Kansas. Grant admires the neon romanticism of Raymond Chandler and the irrational chaos of Mickey Spillane. And he dislikes anything written by Agatha Christie.*

16

Wade the Muddy Waters

By Max Allan Collins

First of all, let's get one thing straight: I am not the killer, nor am I an accomplice. I am, in fact, the one who put the pieces together, as I am, after all, the mystery writer along for the ride. You've not only been inside my head, you've heard directly from me several times on this journey. So you should know two things by now: I didn't kill anybody, and I'm not going to die in this story.

I have withheld some information, yes—but that wasn't dishonesty, just . . . narrative strategy. Writing a nonfiction piece like this isn't easy for me, you know. (You may have noticed me struggling to find just the right voice, which I finally have.) I'm a fiction writer, which is to say a paid liar. This means I may, at times, be a less than trustworthy narrator.

But I assure you I am not lying now. This is the whole, unvarnished truth, nothing but, cross my fingers. I mean, heart.

Okay? Ready to move on? Let's go, then. Specifically, let's
go to the last day of RAGBRAI, in the industrial town of
twenty-some thousand souls known as Muscatine, named
not for the wine, but for an Indian tribe (the Mascoutin
tribe, not the Muscatel). Nestled like a sooty jewel in the
linty navel of the Mississippi—the only portion of those Great
Muddy Waters that runs East and West— Muscatine is famous for watermelons (and musks) and was once known
as the Pearl Button Capital, due to its many pearl button
factories (only one of which is still in existence). The melons aren't really pertinent to our tale—they make only the
slightest cameo appearance (pay attention)—but the pearl
buttons do, I swear, pertain. A little.

That last day of riding—that entire last day, which should
have been the most festive of the event—was a gloomy one.
Not the sky: the sky was properly blue, the grass as green as
the tall corn we glided past. But a pall had been cast by the
murder of that priest.

Oh, nobody official had called it a murder: "accidental
drowning" was the word the Patrol passed along. But it was
clear our killer had shifted M.O.'s on us. Word was the priest
had been snooping, at least until the moment his nostrils
filled up with Iowa City River water. Further, rumor had it,
when the father was dragged ashore, his hair had been parted
and not with a comb.

On our way to Muscatine, I was riding along with Jennie
— but we had a new companion. This skinny, pale, spooky-
eyed character who coughed like a cat and called himself

Ripley was Jennie's new best friend. Or anyway, he was behaving that way, grinning at her, flirting with her in the most archly obnoxious fashion.

"Hotel rooms in Muscatine are going to be golden, tonight," he said, shortly past West Liberty.

The priest's death had not dampened Ripley's spirits.

I knew he wasn't talking to me, but I said, "I suppose you booked ahead?"

"My mighty laptop did. If you need a place to crash, Jennie, I've booked the bridal suite at the Hotel Muscatine. The picture of the hot tub on their web site was delicious."

Jennie didn't reply, and I managed not to puke. What century did this clown crawl out of? Laptop or not, blue spandex be damned, all this pompous idiot lacked was spats and a celluloid collar.

"I, uh, have friends in Muscatine," Jennie said.

"Oh, I do hope you'll reconsider," Ripley said.

"I'll have to take a pass, too," I said. "I got a friend driving me back to Waverly—tempting as that hot tub sounds."

Ripley arched an eyebrow and sneered, and fell into a sullen silence. Which was fine with me and, I could tell, with Jennie.

But Jennie had stayed in her own tent last night, or anyway I assumed so. After she'd wandered off at the Old Cap festivities, I hadn't seen her again till morning when the priest's body was discovered—although I'd looked for her. She couldn't have spent the night with Ichabod Crane here, could she?

We crossed Dougherty Bridge, drifting through quiet farm country, and soon were on Mulberry Street, streaking past a nursing home, a church or two, and a cemetery. That latter would normally not have rated more than a glance—but every biker on this death march had a good gander. A block or so later came an impressive colonial-style funeral home, a hearse just pulling out.

Needless to say, we didn't break into a round of "One Hundred Bottles of Beer on the Wall."

Then we were in a quiet residential area, lovely homes, luxuriant shade trees, soothing sights; and as we rounded a corner, we saw the first signs of locals lining the streets, modest little clusters of kids and parents, waving their hands and sometimes little American flags, whistling and cheering. As we got closer to the downtown, the sidewalks were crowded and the cheering and whistling was washing away the murders from our minds, reminding us this was RAGBRAI, the race that wasn't a race.

Even an aging fossil like yours truly pedaled faster, sat up higher, back arched, feeling like an athlete, including the aching muscles. Finally the flatness of Mulberry dropped off, about the same time the residential area turned commercial; then the Mississippi showed itself, a silvery ribbon at the bottom of the hill, beyond the railroad tracks.

Leaning 'round the corner past the old Elks Lodge, we were in the thick of it now; we were a goddamn parade and kids of all ages were waving and yelling and whistling, like every one of us was coming across the finish line first. Cops held back cars for the important traffic—us—as we wheeled up over the railroad tracks, enjoying the teeth-rattling jar, heading across the parking lot with applause ringing in our ears.

We had begun this journey by dipping our back tires in the Missouri River—and, as was traditional, we ended the trek by dipping our front tires in the Mississippi. Some riders pedaled down the slope of the cement ramp and into the river and went for an impromptu swim; others tossed their bikes in, as if to say good riddance.

I settled for the front tire bit, as did Jennie, and our grinning cadaverous appendage, Ripley.

Riverside Park, normally, was no doubt a quiet, undistinguished patch of grass, broken up by an Indian statue here, a big anchor there, and a bronze Elk on a pedestal that faced the lodge hall across the way. Further north, a rather pitiful playground and a basketball court were dominated by the twin granite pillars that were all that remained of a turn-of-the-century high bridge. The park was unadorned, even shabby, as if the city leaders—worn down by the flooding that consumed this park every few years—had given up.

Today, however, this patchy expanse of park was a mass of sweaty humanity seeking out the tent stands where the Junior Chamber peddled the pedalers pork sandwiches and beer and slices of the fabled local melons. Also doing business was a row of portapotties—or, in RAGBRAI parlance, Kybos (Keep Your Buff Off the Seat).

Ripley was slipping into one of those, while we slipped away from him.

Shortly, Jennie and I stood facing the river, looking across the houseboats in their slips toward the (relatively) recently built high bridge, a characterless span that might have been a railroad bridge, its central archwork like the clenched teeth of a frown. The simple, harsh lines of the bridge lent a starkness, even an ominous quality to an otherwise stunning view.

True, the water nearest us was a muddy green; but, as it stretched to the green-lined horizon of the opposite shore, that color turned to a shimmery blue, the late afternoon sun casting white highlights on its calm surface. To the north, under the bridge, the hazy outline of the locks and dam could be made out. Soon the sun would remind these revelers—those that weren't too drunk to notice, anyway—that Muscatine was home to the most beautiful sunrises and sunsets in the world, according to one former resident named Samuel Clemens.

"Breathtaking," Jennie said quietly.

I slipped my hand in hers. "Is something wrong? Want to talk?"

"Nothing. No."

I didn't push it.

The local high school jazz band—doing some respectable swing, jump, jiving and wailing —was playing up on the cement platform at the far end of the park. The crowd, most of it anyway, gathered there to listen and to dance. Between songs, that woman from the *Register*, Charlie whatever-the-hell-her-name-was, oversaw closing ceremonies, thanking the participants, particularly "in the face of this week's tragedies."

Then she introduced Lt. Scott Dallas, the trooper in charge of the murder investigation. The lanky, raw-boned lawman stepped up to the mike and spoke with quiet confidence— no one-two-one-two testing. He was ready to go.

"I would like to thank you for your patience," Dallas said. The mike fed back, but Dallas didn't blink at the squeal. "It's been a long, difficult, grueling week . . . even for a RAGBRAI."

This stirred a ripple of nervous laughter. Dallas frowned, not intending levity. "As you know, we've had to keep close tabs on you riders, and you may be hearing from us again. We have your names and numbers. Don't be alarmed if or when we call. It would be impractical and unkind to keep you here tonight. Please understand that further interrogation of a number of you will be necessary in the coming days and perhaps weeks."

Jennie and I were standing almost directly in front of Dallas, but well back in the crowd. I sensed something to my right and noticed a pair of troopers pushing through, parting the biker bodies like Moses at the Red Sea.

A beefy trooper in his forties stopped before us—the name plate on his shirt said HASSELL—and said, "Ms. Wyman, if you'll come with me, please."

Jennie's face showed no emotion—she might have been carved from ivory. Finally, she nodded, and I said, "I'm coming with her."

"Mr. Wade, that's fine with us. We have some questions for you, too."

And we went with them, the wide eyes of the murmuring crowd glued to us.

At the south end of the riverfront sat a red brick building with a green roof, a single tall pitched-roofed story, a refurbished train station that served as Muscatine's activity and tourism center. The State Patrol had commandeered this facility, the Pearl Street Station, as their Muscatine base of operations.

We went up a handful of well-worn wooden steps and trouped around the building's deck, past a plaque that indicated the record flood crest (it came up to my nose). I held Jennie's hand as we skirted the building. Shell-shocked as she was, she didn't notice the quaint surroundings: benches in recessed bricked lounging areas, shrubs spotted around expertly, old-fashioned streetlamps standing mute watch, the entryway to an asphalt bike path that provided RAGBRAI types like us an incredible view of the Mississippi as we pedaled away.

But we weren't pedaling away, we were being rounded up like cattle into the side door of the Pearl City Station. The interior was just more bricks and a cement floor and banquet-style tables (a kitchen was at one end—the facility was apparently used for weddings and the like). The ceiling was chapel high and our footsteps—and, later, our words—echoed.

The big room was empty but for another patrol man—

that good-looking blond Tom Cruise-ish kid named Lars Loving, who'd abandoned his racing togs for a State Patrol uniform—and our friend Ripley, seated at one of the banquet tables like a pouty kid being kept after school.

The windows were open, letting a nice breeze into the un-airconditioned building.

Dallas was ushering us toward the table where Ripley sat, when Jennie blurted, "I did it! I killed him! I killed Tom . . . ."

Just like the end of Perry Mason.

Well, I had figured she'd killed the bastard, and didn't much care: Eyepatch, had he survived, was hardly a candidate for RAGBRAI's Mr. Congeniality award.

But I also figured there was a lot more to this—because this young woman, whom I had fallen in love with on first silly sight—was in no way capable of the other grotesque murders that had taken place on this ill-fated excursion.

Soon I was seated next to Jennie, with Ripley and Dallas right across from us. Loving, Hassell and another trooper, a paunchy character whose nametag read ZENITH, hovered.

"Ms. Wyman," Dallas said, softly, gently, kindly, "you have the right to remain silent . . . ." When the litany was complete, Dallas added, ever so casually, "Maybe you'd like to tell us about it."

She did. I had a feeling Dallas knew a lot of it already, but the satisfaction in his narrowing eyes said he liked hearing it firsthand from her.

When she had joked to Eyepatch, "Wasn't I married to

you?" it had been no joke. Back in Joliet, Spurgeon—a prison guard—had been an abusive husband to Jennie. Standing up for herself one time, she had once almost put his eye out—almost. He had worn an eyepatch for months, healing up . . . and when he showed up on RAGBRAI, stalking her, that eyepatch was a signal, a warning . . . .

"No, not a warning," Jennie said, eyes liquid, "a threat . . . a promise."

She had divorced him, and had not seen him in years. He had gone into the witness protection program after informing on other guards at the prison where he worked, and she had assumed she would never see him again— which would have been none too soon.

That first night of RAGBRAI, she had gone to Spurgeon, begging him to leave her alone, and he had laughed at her, threatened her with one of his pearl-handled knives . . . and she had grabbed it from him, scuffled with him, and plunged it into his chest.

Jennie was weeping now. I slipped an arm around her.

Dallas waited—he was a decent man, Dallas—but then, as he must, asked, "What then, Ms. Wyman?"

"Then," she said with a shrug, "I just ran away."

"You didn't stick those knives in his eyes?"

She shuddered. "No! No. I could never do such a thing."

Dallas twitched a non-smile. "Ms. Wyman, only you had a motive to cover up that murder, and make it look as though the Eye Doctor had done it. . . .With your background in criminology, you certainly would have known the M.O. of

Iowa's most famous serial killer."

I said, "Just because she studied criminology in college, doesn't make her—"

Dallas raised an eyebrow. "Ms. Wyman is a former guard in several penal institutions—Joliet, in Illinois, though she wasn't involved in the scandal there, and Ft. Madison, here in Iowa."

Jennie sat forward. Her eyes, though damp, had strength in them now. "I didn't cover up Tom's . . . death. I would have come forward, after I composed myself, if someone . . . someone else hadn't taken it upon themselves to cover up for me. Why whoever-did-this did this, I have no idea! After all, I had nothing to hide! I was guilty of nothing more than defending myself from a sick stalker, an abusive husband who was going O.J. on me that very moment!"

I patted her shoulder, but my eyes were on Dallas. "There's another clue you might want to consider, lieutenant—a little obscure, but a clue: those pearl handles."

"What about them?" Dallas asked.

I answered his question by posing one to Jennie: "Where were you and Spurgeon originally from?"

"Why we . . . we both come from right here in Muscatine. He was a deputy sheriff, and I met him then."

I nodded, gave her a supportive gaze. "Is your family, by any chance, the Wymans who once owned a pearl button factory here?"

"Yes . . . and you're right, Jim. Those pearl handles were for my benefit. For the meaning they would have in my

eyes . . . in whatever sense you want to take that phrase . . .
a special signature Tom could sign that the real serial killer
couldn't."

Silence draped the brick chamber; if you strained, you
could make out the muffled sound of festivities, distant as
a fading memory.

"Ms. Wyman," Dallas said, "I wish I could believe you. I
want to believe you. But we have other murders here. And
something very . . . don't mean to step on your turf, Mr.
Wade, but . . . diabolical afoot. Somehow, someone attracted
a serial killer here to help cover up the murder of Tom
Spurgeon. That would require a very special kind of sociopath, a sophisticated sociopath, capable of orchestrating these
various killings."

My mind was racing. I was no cop—no detective. But I
was a mystery writer.

"What," I said, almost demanded, "is he doing here?"
And I thrust my finger at the sullen Ripley: Uncle Wade
Wants You.

"Why don't I ask you a question, first?" Dallas said. "The
question that explains what you're doing here—how do you
account for the coincidence of your work echoing these murders, past and present?"

Stubbornly, I said, "I'll be glad to answer that—after you
tell me: why Ripley?"

"Mr. Ripley is here because, according to the cell phone
records of Tom Spurgeon, the last phone call our victim
made was to a number belonging to Mr. Ripley, although

'Ripley' is not his real name."

Now it clicked.

"I didn't think it was," I said. "Lt. Dallas, would you mind humoring me, briefly? You have a confession to Spurgeon's killing from Ms. Wyman . . . but you don't have the right man for the other murders. Would you mind listening to this mystery writer spin a yarn?"

Folding his arms, quietly amused, Dallas leaned back in his folding chair and said, "Spin away."

"Mr. Ripley here thinks he's cute, very cute. He's a mystery fan himself, you know—professes to like my books, but I don't think he has what it takes to understand my craft. At any rate, our mystery buff has joined RAGBRAI under an assumed name—Ripley. Pat Ripley. 'Pat' is for Patricia Highsmith, a noted author of suspense, and 'Ripley' is for Highsmith's famous character: a killer. A murderer who always gets away with it."

Ripley was smiling now; his mouth was, anyway — his eyes weren't.

"Just for fun," I said, "let's presume that the business 'Ripley' maintains in Denver, the clients he keeps in touch with via laptop and cell phone, the contract work he does . . . is contract murder."

Ripley, still smiling, said, "Really, lieutenant—do I have to listen to this drivel?"

"No," Dallas said, sitting forward. "Pay no attention, if you prefer. Me, I'm gonna listen with both ears open."

"Let's not forget," I said, "who brought the twin knives

to the party, the pearl-handed switch blades that wound up in Tom Spurgeon's eyes: Tom Spurgeon himself. What if Tom Spurgeon—who went out of his way not to mention in front of anyone that he had been married to Jennie, here—had planned to kill Jennie in just the manner to which we've all become accustomed: utilizing the Eye Doctor's M.O."

"But Ms. Wyman killed Spurgeon before he could do that," Dallas said.

"Exactly," I said. "And suppose Spurgeon—who wanted to kill his ex-wife himself, who wanted to savor the revenge of that act—had hired in advance Mr. Ripley, here, the contract killer, to throw in a few copycat killings, to muddy the waters (if you'll pardon the expression) and provide Spurgeon with an alibi."

"If I am this sinister contract killer," Ripley said, "why would I commit these copycat murders after my employer was dead?"

"Because," I said, "like most contract killers, you go through a middle man, a broker—or your client will approach you him- or herself, but under an assumed name, and never in person—by e-mail or phone, perhaps, as you did with Spurgeon . . . but you wouldn't be able to identify him, wouldn't know the murder motive, wouldn't in fact know anything that could lead the cops to him should you be caught."

Dallas was nodding. Ripley was still smiling, shaking his head at this "nonsense."

From behind me, Lars Loving asked, "How do you explain the coincidence of the real Eye Doctor showing up?"

"I can do that," I said, "by first explaining the coincidence of how the Eye Doctor's M.O. made it into my books." And I told them how I had used the real-life serial killer's killing style in my fiction. "The *Register* did an advance story on RAGBRAI, with sidebars on several celebrity bikers, myself included, and in particular played up my participation big, having fun with the idea of a mystery writer, who writes about tough guys, having to get 'tough' himself and pedal his ass off. In so many words."

"I saw that article," Dallas said.

"So did the real Eye Doctor. I think he came on RAGBRAI to rub my nose in his murders—and maybe put me away, murder me for 'exploiting' him and his hobby. But, fortunately, lieutenant, you killed him before he could kill me."

"This is all preposterous," Ripley said. And he stood, and pointed a finger at Jennie, accusingly. "All I know is I witnessed that woman killing the eyepatched man . . . and it didn't look like self-defense to me."

"Sit down," Dallas said, quietly.

Swallowing, Ripley did.

"Mr. Ripley," I said, "if you witnessed that 'murder,' why didn't you come forward at the time?"

"Well, I, uh . . ."

"Perhaps, as a contract killer, you preferred not to call attention to yourself. Or perhaps you saw it as an opportunity. Maybe that's why you thrust those knives into the eyes of the man who, unbeknownst to you, had hired you . . . but who you'd never met . . . turning this murder into one of the Eye Doctor kills you'd been hired to concoct."

Now it was Jennie who was standing, pointing her finger at Ripley. "He tried to blackmail me into having sex with him last night! He killed that priest, then threatened me with a knife, held it high over his head, and said I had until tonight to change my attitude . . . . He didn't like being with women who couldn't 'appreciate his charm,' he said."

"That's a damn lie!" Ripley said, and he too stood.

I remained seated. "Well, it was just a story . . . a yarn I spun, another wild one from Iowa's resident mystery writer. You're right, Mr. Ripley—probably just a bunch of bunk. But Lt. Dallas, perhaps you might consider holding Mr. Ripley here until you've had a chance to check out his background in Denver, and investigate that 'business' of his."

And Ripley, hands clamped onto the edge of the banquet table, upturned it, shoving it over, and onto Jennie and me, taking Zenith and Hassell down, too. Dallas rose, but Ripley, with savage swiftness, grabbed onto the trooper's ears and brought the man's head down into Ripley's upthrust knee.

Dallas tumbled to the cement and was on his back, groggy, when Ripley yanked the .38 revolver from the trooper's holster. Ripley trained it on the other troopers, who were on the floor, except for Loving, whose hands were in the air.

Then Ripley jumped through the nearest window. Loving went out the side door.

By the time I got out from under the table and was outside the chase was under way: Ripley was on his golden bike, pedaling up that asphalt bike path, and the lean trooper was taking off after him on the Huffy.

Ripley's mountain bike was far superior to the starter bicycle the young trooper rode, but Loving was an athlete, a kid in top shape, and within seconds he had overtaken Ripley, pulling around in front of him, sending the contract killer and his golden wheels tumbling down the embankment toward the river.

The golden bike plunged into the water, sinking, bobbing back to the surface, thanks to its tires. Its owner was still on the shore, barely. With an animal look replacing the would-be sophistication of the mask he'd worn, Ripley raised the confiscated .38 toward Loving.

But the young trooper fired first—one, two, three whipcracks, splitting the air, hardly noticed by the crowd way down in the park.

The three shots shook the skinny Ripley, shook him like a naughty child, picked up and hurled him back, with a splash, into the river, where the muddy waters turned a thin crimson as the clever man floated on his back, staring at approaching night with eyes already overtaken by that longest, darkest night.

Dallas, not even touching his bloodied head, was shambling up the asphalt bike path toward Loving, who stared numbly down at the corpse he'd just created. The older cop placed a hand on the younger cop's shoulder and whispered words of praise and support that caused Loving to nod and even smile, a little.

Jennie was at my side, and then my arm was around her. "We shouldn't waste it, you know," I said.

"Waste what?" She asked, eyes bright but no longer wet.

"That hotel room that asshole booked. With the hot tub. I'm sweaty and hot and my muscles ache. And ol' Ripley sure as hell won't be needing it tonight."

She blinked. "But . . . surely I'm to be arrested . . . ."

"The lieutenant knows it was self-defence. I bet I can talk him into turning you over into my custody. You don't mind being in my custody, do you?"

Then she began to laugh. It was just threatening to turn hysterical, when she said, "Tough guy."

Then I kissed her. And you thought Tom Cruise was going to get the girl.

MAX ALLEN COLLINS *has won the "Best Novel" Shamus award from the Private Eye Writers of America twice, for* True Detective *(1983) and* Stolen Away *(1991), both entries in his cycle of historical novels about detective Nathan Heller.*

The Heller novels hold the record for Shamus nominations (9); the latest is Majic Man, *in which the Chicago P.I. "solves" the enigma of the Roswell Incident. Since 1973, Collins has published 50 novels, most of them in the mystery/suspense field, as well as a number of nonfiction works. (He has been nominated for the Mystery Writers of America "Edgar" for both fiction and nonfiction).*

From 1977 to 1993, Collins wrote the internationally syndicated Dick Tracy *comic strip, and has written both the* Batman *comic book and strip; he is the co-creator of the comic book properties* Ms. Tree, Wild Dog, Johnny Dynamite: Underworld *and* Mike Danger, *and his 1998 graphic novel* Road to Perdition, *has been optioned by Dreamworks. A* New York Times *bestselling writer, Collins is perhaps the top author of movie tie-novels, having penned such bestsellers as* In The Line of Fire, Air Force One, Waterworld, The Mummy *and* Saving Private Ryan, *as well as two* NYPD Blue *novels for Steven Bochco.*

In recent years Collins has turned his hand to independent film and video productions. His black-comedy thrillers Mommy *and* Mommy's Day *are cult favorites and recently appeared as* DVD *collectors' editions; his 1998 documentary* Mike Hammer's Mickey Spillane—*which won the Iowa Motion Picture Association "Award of Excellence" for best television program—was invited to the Festival in Noir in Courmayeur, Italy, for a screening out of competition, and by the British Film Institute for a screening in July 1999 at the National Film Theatre in London. Collins is serving his second year as president of the Iowa Motion Picture Association.*

Epilogue

Bellevue, September 2010

By Richard, Lord Acton

Chief Inspector Reginald Brontey-Blemmings of Scotland Yard, impeccably dressed in a light grey Savile Row suit, sat on a bench in Bellevue, Iowa. He gazed at the Mississippi as he listened to Jim Wade tell the story of the RAGBRAI murders. They had become e-mail friends some years before when Jim was writing a book on the Westminster Ripper—a serial killer who had disemboweled several members of Parliament before Brontey-Blemmings had arrested him. The Chief Inspector had just been a guest speaker at a law-and-order conference in Chicago. On an impulse, he had rented a car and driven to Iowa to meet Jim for the first time. Bellevue—chosen for its charm—was their rendezvous.

A decade earlier, Jim Wade had been balding and slightly overweight. Now, still balding, he had put on 30 pounds and, in T-shirt and shorts, seemed a curious contrast to his trim, smartly dressed companion. As he described the RAGBRAI murders, Jim periodically munched on a doughnut.

Brontey-Blemmings sat erect, listening intently. When Jim reached the end of his account, the Chief Inspector sighed, turned to him, and said: "But you didn't get the girl, did you, Jim?"

"Nope. The cops arrested Jennie for the murder of Eyepatch as we took our first step toward the Hotel Muscatine."

"What was the outcome?"

"The cops didn't buy her story of self-defense. In the end, the prosecutor agreed to a plea of voluntary manslaughter. She did five years in the women's prison at Mitchelville and then was released."

"And you were waiting for her?"

"Yup," said Jim. "But she wasn't waiting for me." He laughed. "She didn't get Tom Cruise, either, but she did go for a hunk. That great, useless, hairy, blond beast, Thor of the Marvelaires. The pair of them are living down on his farm near Villisca." He reached for another doughnut. "Poor old Jennie. Spending her life polishing Thor's stupid axe."

Jim offered a greasy sack to Brontey-Blemmings. "Have a doughnut, Reggie."

"Thank you, but I would prefer a good pot of tea. However, first I have some more questions. What happened to the original Captain America?"

"That nut," said Jim. "The real Eye Doctor had come to him with a story that he wanted the Captain America get-up to play a trick on some RAGBRAI friends. He offered $200 for the costume and for him to lie low. Cap One took off for Chicago and then went back to Madison County."

He laughed. "But he was no Clint Eastwood."

"How do you mean?"

"Cap One had an unheroic end to his biking career. The Marvelaires got together for the next RAGBRAI. Cap One tried some crazy stunt, flew over the handlebars, and broke both legs. The other three heroes—in full comic-book gear—formed an honor guard and followed his ambulance to the hospital on their bikes. That was the last ride of the Marvelaires."

Brontey-Blemmings reflected. "From what you have told me, the real Eye Doctor—Captain America the Second—murdered Jennie's friend Angi Gales and, as his charming trademark, cut out her tongue."

"Yup."

"Well," said the Chief Inspector. "What about the other two murders? Ripley drowned the priest and presumably killed Kristen Jensen, the television reporter. Why did he choose those two?"

"I've thought about that," said Jim. "If you're a sicko like Ripley, you crave publicity, max publicity. Believe me, in this country the murder of a correspondent for NBC's *Today Show* guarantees media frenzy. The priest was just frosting on the cake to feed the media."

"We British say 'icing on the cake'," said Brontey-Blemmings. "All right, I will have a doughnut after all. Now tell me about the other people. What happened to that demi-god of a policeman, Lars Loving? Did he get involved with Charlie Andropolous, the young woman who wrote for the

Des Moines Register?"

"No, Charlie had her eye on someone else. As for Lars—hang on to your hat, Reggie—he's ridden the last few RAGBRAIs in Team Fatherhood."

"I say, what can you mean?"

"Well, it seems that after being hit by a semi and pumping Ripley full of lead, old Lars got religion. He traded the State Patrol for a seminary, and today he's Father Lars Loving of Dubuque."

"Mysterious are the ways of the Lord," said the Chief Inspector. "Who was it that caught Charlie's fancy?"

"None other than lean, raw-boned Lieutenant Scott Dallas."

"Goodness gracious. Did she have a thing about policemen?"

"Her mother was the first female agent with the old Iowa Bureau of Criminal Investigation—so maybe her love of cops was hereditary." Jim continued, "Anyway, Charlie upped and sold her bed and breakfast in Bella, moved to Des Moines, and married the lieutenant. She still writes pieces for the *Register* when she isn't looking after their three kids. They haven't been seen at RAGBRAI since."

Brontey-Blemmings removed the handkerchief from his top pocket and carefully dusted crumbs from his elegant knees. He contemplated the river. "How quaint that the RAGBRAI bicyclists always dip their front wheels in the Mississippi," he mused. Then he furrowed his brow. "By the way, what effect did the murders have on RAGBRAI?"

"Best publicity any bike ride ever had. People are thrilled by murder. The number of riders has doubled in the last ten years, and now there are bikers from more than 40 countries."

"Jim, you have answered nearly all of my questions. But what about you?"

"I still write mysteries. I've given up on women—or they on me, and I never want to go near RAGBRAI again."

The expanse of the Mississippi and the Indian summer's day made Brontey-Blemmings think that the Thames was only a silver snake, a wintry snake sometimes bound in mist and fog. The fog took his mind to Victorian London, Sherlock Holmes, and Dr. Watson.

"One final point," he said. "You saw a dog run from Eyepatch's tent. Dogs in murder inquiries have fascinated me ever since I first read Conan Doyle's 'Silver Blaze.' You surely must know that story, Jim?"

"Remind me."

"The inspector says to Sherlock Holmes: 'Is there any point to which you would wish to draw my attention?'

'To the curious incident of the dog in the night-time,' replies Holmes.

'The dog did nothing in the night-time.'

'That was the curious incident,' says Holmes." Brontey-Blemmings went on: "So will you enlighten me about the behavior of the Eyepatch dog?"

"Look, Reggie," said Jim, "that dog had a rough evening. He crawls into Eyepatch's tent and cozies up to him. Then a woman comes in, scuffles with his pal and kills him. Next a man comes in and pokes knives into his pal's eyes. Then the tent catches on fire. Whatever an English dog would do under those circumstances, an Iowa dog does not stick around looking curious. He runs . . . and that's exactly what this dog did."

"Quite right," said Chief Inspector Reginald Brontey-Blemmings. "And now, let's go and find that pot of tea."

RICHARD ACTON *is a former English barrister who is married to an Iowan. He divides his life between London, where he is a member of the House of Lords, and Cedar Rapids, where he is a writer. His most recent book is* A Brit Among the Hawkeyes. *He has written many articles on Iowa history, and he and his wife, Patricia Nassif Acton, wrote the award-winning* To Go Free: A Treasury of Iowa's Legal Heritage. *Acton has contributed to numerous periodicals, including the* New York Times Book Review, North American Review, Christian Science Monitor, Des Moines Register, Mystery Scene, *and (in England),* The Literary Review, The Economist, *and* The Spectator. *He loves Sherlock Holmes and hates bicycling.*

BARBARA LOUNSBERRY *loves biking, but has never been on RAGBRAI. (She is afraid of crowds.) She is a professor of English at the University of Northern Iowa and is the author or editor of four books:* The Art of Fact: Contemporary Artists of Nonfiction *(1990);* The Writer in You *(1992);* Writing Creative Nonfiction: The Literature of Reality, *co-edited with bestselling writer Gay Talese (1996); and* The Tales We Tell: Perspectives on the Short Story, *co-edited with Stephen Pett of Iowa State University, Susan Lohafer of the University of Iowa, and R. C. Feddersen, a former UNI graduate student, (1998). Barbara received UNI's Distinguished Scholar Award in 1994 and was chosen UNI's Outstanding Teacher in 1998. Her husband, John, teaches elementary physical education in Waterloo, and rode on Team Mary in RAGBRAI 1999.*

KIM BEHM *has been a Senior Illustrator with Hellman and Associates in Cedar Falls since 1979. He received his BFA and MA from the University of New Mexico. His paintings have appeared in exhibitions since 1965. He was born in Des Moines and currently lives in Cedar Falls with his wife Gretchen and two children. Kim is a member of the KUNI Friends Board of Directors and bicycles regularly.*

Amy Roach *is a graphic designer at The University of Iowa where she has designed award-winning publications for the past 13 years. She graduated with honors from Illinois State University in 1983. Amy lives in Cedar Rapids with her husband and three children. She hasn't ridden a bike in years but is certain she can remember how.*

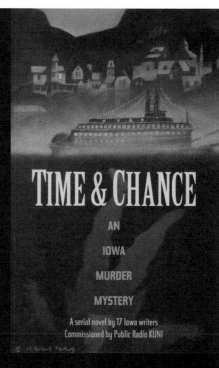